COMFORT FOR THE AFFLICTED

A Deranged Christmas

A Novella

By

D.S. Ayars

Printed in the United States of America

First Printing, 2021

Paperback ISBN: 978-0-578-85290-4
eBook ISBN: 978-0-578-85291-1

Contents

Preface 7

Chapter One: Weather Report 11

Chapter Two: There Was a Time 15

Chapter Three: Those Wonderfully Weird Moments 21

Chapter Four: Mutant Solidarity 31

Chapter Five: Easy Writer 37

Chapter Six: Grace 43

Chapter Seven: Vanity 53

Chapter Eight: The Preacher 59

Chapter Nine: Clark 65

Chapter Ten: Comfort for the Afflicted 69

Chapter Eleven: Over the Hill 81

Chapter Twelve: Then It Gets Strange 91

Chapter Thirteen: Merry Catharsis. 99

Chapter Fourteen: The Letter 103

INCLUDED SHORT STORIES:

Lost at the Bar: Confessions of the Drunk and Stupid 107

BellaRae: Quiet Please, Psychedelic Session in Progress. 125

Acknowledgements: Great Thanks to the Honor Roll:. 141

In Memory of:

Clark Ayars, Dick Wild, and Lou Drew

I had the Privileged Honor of standing on the shoulders of these Giants.

AND

Dedicated to:

My whole Fam-damly. I Love the hell out of each One of you high powered Heroes.

Preface

Legend has it, the universe has nothing but good intentions for you. Similarly, I have also been rebuked, God wants only what's best for me. In other words, a weird chunk of our strung-out lives tends to work out in varying strange and twisted ways. Everything seems to work-out for the best, regardless of what one may or may not embrace as sacred and true.

It all seems to remain a rich and robust, dry hump of a mystery (not to everyone, though). But to an unfortunate preponderance of Homo-sapiens, this all continues to be some sort of fucked-up, nefarious joke, or even an elitist secret if you'd like. Because as it stands sex, drugs, rock-n-roll; politics, religion, the universe, the fifth dimension and all other desperate escapades hold no obligation toward anybody's comprehension. But it is a curious thing when one strives for and achieves what he or she wants, and yet, some undetected gnawing-curse fiendishly leeches on to the blessing.

These frenzied mosh-pits, through the impishly torrent waves of life, compel us to continue moving forward toward smooth and more friendly waters. A climate which affords us a fresh, deep sigh of relief. A safer, kinder place where we might liberate our death grip from the broken-down helm, rest our burdened shoulders, take down our deflated sails and absorb the sudden beauty we have been overlooking, while stuck in our fierce rage of reprise for this reprieve. And sure, all this may strike you as a bunch of generalized, lofty gibberish.

And it could very well be. Yet, we still need details because we want answers. Lots of them. The bottom-line. What's the point? If there is a point, right? And so, it stands, the devil slithers incognito in the details where no sympathy rests for any rotten bastard. When we do find that fucker, we get answers. Ugly ones. As a result, we are more cynical, perhaps even wiser. Uncertain, to be sure, but perspective, nonetheless.

Despite that, in those transient moments when we get to indulge in the spinning yarn of somebody else's atrocious story, we catch a brief break. A sinister pardon of reckless abandon from our own putrid shit. The weekend rendezvous from the mundane jerks and shoves of our daily justifications and excuses. Our cherished reasons why, and why not.

It is an astonishing chronicle, in which I've been commissioned to allocate for any passerby to behold these hideous accounts right before keen eyes. Never-mind clinging to trivial comforts just in case there's a need to bail-out quickly, the less luggage the better the ride. For this fabrication might get a trite stupefying, even offensively absurd to the witness, hold fast all fortitude and courage. Because at face-value, William P. Hyneezitzs (retired, clinical psychologist) appears inadequate, unpresentable, awkward and down-right boring to anybody who meets the good Doctor.

Our mediocre mental health healer has experienced a rather insanely weird and spectacular life. A solid-gold, painful pleasure, teeming with twisted turns, strange styling and jarring jolts. Dr. Hyneezitzs grew up in a comfortable, decent home. A pleasant home of two sophisticated, attentive parents. Growing up, William had no discernable odds stacked against him. Educated with the best higher learning money and overbearing (loving) parents could buy; our eager psychologist arduously moved forward in a prosperous career, and a successful family of his own. William is blessed with a stunning professional wife and five well nurtured children who now enjoy their own attainments and achievements. Without question, these days the doctor appears, a comfortably retired family-man who holds no detectable signs of an unusual and electrifying existence.

But make no mistake, William P. Hyneezitzs has a bewitching tale to tell. An account so beguiling and disturbing, the likes of which could very well derange the most skillful of psychologists. Beware of getting too hung-up on the fantasy, though; for as the great mind C. G. Jung, whom with brilliant, penetrating insight wrote, "It is, in fact, one of the most important tasks of psychic hygiene to pay continual attention to the symptomatology of unconscious contents and processes, for the Good Reason that the conscious mind is always in danger of becoming one-sided, of keeping to well-worn paths and getting stuck in blind alleys." On this note, as the weathered atheists used to say in times of dehumanizing-doom and mind-altering mockery, "Godspeed."

CHAPTER ONE
Weather Report

"It seems hardly proper to write of life without once mentioning happiness; so we shall let the reader answer this question for himself: who is the happier man, he who has braved the storm of life and lived, or he who has stayed securely on shore and merely existed" (Dr. Gonzo).

Like a senseless fool I bought this top-of-the-line snow shovel and just as I was en route to grab the nice toasty gloves I needed, I got locked into a shadowy memory. One which gripped me deep enough, I'd mechanically leave the old hardware store with a newly purchased shovel, and no gloves. Again. It's fucking freezing out here and I haven't had a decent pair of gloves all winter. I obsessively tell myself to focus and be present. Yet even this uninspired mantra triggers my daunting affliction, some sort of eerie nostalgia. I chase ghosts who burn me to ashes and take my thoughts hostage by the rueful echoes which haunt the vast reaches of my humiliated mind.

I have no reason, nor excuse for this sort of addiction. Nobody can really discern my fantastic infatuation, because of my affect affording a disposition of being friendly and somewhat flaccid. Amongst family and friends, I silently panic to resuscitate my concentration from being choked out by the ghastly hands of the oddities I've experienced, and the wonderfully weird observations I've encountered. It is a vast and layered life I have been cursed to be blessed with. Still, I should know better, I am a psychologist.

Damn, it's cold! My hands are turning purple, and I haven't even started shoveling this daunting driveway. Here I am a retired psychologist; it's three days before my birthday, my kids are on their way over to stay with us through the Christmas weekend, and I'm scavenging for some reasonable focus as though I were one of my old patients.

BellaRae's out of my league, but my diligent wife will get me through this perverse, big-birthday-bash. In part, this craziness is because my over-privileged parents were fortuitous enough to govern the day, I was to spew out onto this spinning twisted terra—December twenty-fifth, nineteen fifty-five. They, with convincing conviction, insisted this made me special (which by association made them special too). And indeed, my mother and father made damned sure I felt that way. My childhood was too good to be true. Now, this tradition continues upon the brooding shoulders of my wife BellaRae, and her stellar abilities to serve the same codependency to our over-privileged children. We, too, are control freaks. In fact, our kids (who are adults now) are due to arrive soon enough for a fun weekend chalked full of tender talks, loving accolades, and savage sporting on my dreary persona.

In the meantime, my beloved will bestir this monotonous meeting into a magical reflection we all get to soak our feet in on any given dreary day. Mrs. Hyneezitzs is a semi-retired psychiatrist who utilizes high powered tools, such as psilocybin, MDMA, LSD, DMT, along with outstanding skill in these therapies. She specializes in sex therapy. A Proverbs 31, attentive mother, and a top-of-the line, spectacular partner. BellaRae Josephine Hyneez-itzs is a champion in living life. And make no mistake, I never get bored.

Hey, I made it to the mailbox. I think I've been shoveling this driveway for approximately thirty years now, here in beautiful Coeur d' Alene, Idaho. There's BellaRae with an arresting smile and a flirting sly wink, waving at me through the front picture window. The radiance of her authentic delight melts my cold cynicism all the time. But as I raise my numbed, purple hand to wave back; she rolls her eyes and infectiously laughs herself into a red face of tickled tears, knowing damned well why I have no gloves. She knows me inside-out, upside-down, and all around. I chuckle too.

The radiant warmth which fills the cold air, because of our deep connection, reminds me of the paralyzing crush I had on BellaRae the first time I indirectly met her in college. It wasn't until 1976, when we went on our first date. I have never been the same since. I have a good life. Unfortunately, I struggle to let go of the past and not obsess on things I could have done differently. I still overthink myself into disabling embarrassment with things I could have done better years ago.

CHAPTER TWO
There Was a Time

"And then the day came when the risk to remain tight in a bud was greater than the risk it took to bloom" (Anais Nin).

A storm of reminiscence overtakes my mind considering how smoothly Mrs. Hyneezitzs (or B.J., as she was fondly monikered in college) took my heart, mind, and body hostage with her stupefying beauty and her bewitching ways. Her methods had the enticing, potent flavor of darkness; yet, she was too angelic to be iniquitous. Some things never change. We didn't officially meet until graduate school, though; that is, at the University of California, in Berkeley. I was poised to attend the University of California, in L.A.; but my desires for B.J. became all-consuming, and unfortunately an unsympathetic deception. Through my non-threatening disposition, friendly smile, and an obliging ear, I slighted information on where the future Mrs. Hyneezitzs would earn her masters in psychiatry.

It was the befriending of BellaRae's desperate loudmouthed friend (Suzy Sowschitts), and the liberties afforded me through my parents having the right connections and the proper finances. The entitlement and the upper-class status Suzy and I had in common were the low-brow, plastic bullshit similarities to kick off our fraudulent friendship. I'd seen BellaRae in most of my classes throughout college. For me, it was 'love at first sight'. It also didn't take me long to notice that this sassy slut was also in every fucking class, right next to B.J.. Literally. Everywhere BellaRae went, there was Suzy. Suzy was impetuously needy and annoying. Like a rapacious parasite, she leeched on and gorged herself with as much of B.J.'s powers of attraction as she could. But then again, everybody seemed enthralled with BellaRae Josephine Johnson.

At any rate, I had to follow BellaRae; I could, so I did. B.J. (I discovered, via a study group Suzy hosted) rented a room from Sowschitts. Suzy's unavailable parents bought, and deeply paid for anything she wanted, if it didn't require time and attention. Suzy rigorously attempted to pass herself off as a debutante. She was, as awful as it may seem, only offal for us cowardly bottom-feeders. I regarded her as my greasy ticket in getting closer to BellaRae. Therefore, I quickly befriended Sowschitts under the cruel guise of time and attention.

I invested a good preponderance of my college days at Suzy's lofty condo, tolerating her boring facades and dramatic fabrications; and all this insanity just to find-out and capture BellaRae's interest. It's not that Suzy was physically unappealing, quite the contrary, it was who and what she was. She was a plastic monument to a long-forgotten, throwaway society. Every disrespectful and grotesque jerk-off used her. We all secretly loathed her, except for BellaRae. B.J. always did, and obviously always will be a genuine friend to the odd and unacceptable.

BellaRae and I had the same classes and attended all the same study groups, yet there were no significant interactions (eye contact, conversations, flirting, et-cetera) until Berkeley. It obsessed me. My own illusions of who she might be confined me, and how I might be a part of her world. A few of the social obstacles I had in soliciting BellaRae's regard were that I'm not entirely captivating, outspoken, or handsome. Subsequently, 'til this very day I typically live through others and tell their stories, as though they are mine. Pitifully, I rely on those who surround me to feed my insatiable neediness.

However, when one is suddenly an alien in a strange land, even the merely recognizable may seem like an old friend. The first day of Berkeley was the strange land, and BellaRae was the alien. Not to mention, I'm recognizable. Nobody else from college was there. It was down to her and me. All I had to do was intrude with a familiar, albeit disappointing, smiling face looking for her greeting. We were in the admission's line when I finally gathered enough self-destructive desperation so I could physically captivate BellaRae's attention.

After I dramatically threw myself to the ground, I then feverishly tossed my paperwork and pretentious books up into the anxious air. Also, I screamed and cursed God like I'd seriously injured myself. Most of the good-minded folks in the building gathered around me with concern, asking me if I was alright, and if I were "in need of medical attention." Others were collecting my unnecessary mess with polite civility. Amid this hair-brained chaos, my ears turned pink and perked up when I heard BellaRae hysterically laughing at the pathetic theater.

Finally, after sustaining enough oxygen in her lungs (amongst the amusement) she cried out, "Is that you, Hyneezitzs?" Her musings were intoxicating. She handed me my thick-framed, thick-lensed glasses which had somehow landed directly before her feet during the concocted collapse. The crowd went from public compassion to tearful—with all fingers pointing at an idiot—mirth. BellaRae then wiped the streaming tears from her radiant cheeks and gestured to help me up.

The gaiety faded to embarrassing giggles and whispers, when admissions called my name, "William Pops Hyneezitzs, you're next!" Everybody, especially BellaRae, folded over into a deeper laugh. Including the admissions clerk. What self-esteem? And so, what? I had B.J.'s notice, a flimsy shelter in a lonely land.

I moved forward with my awkward walk of glee and shame, to the front desk where one gets handed the rest of their life on a slip of paper. Upon arrival, I started getting somewhat comfortable with my feats of humiliation, because Miss Johnson walked with me, which more than helped. Along the way, she arrested my clumsy theater with a friendly, "Meet me in the front of this building this evening, around six. I'll buy us something to eat, while you lick your wounds." I became overwhelmed with excitement as she kissed me on the cheek, broke-away and with a wink got back into the laughing line. And there began my clearest opportunity of getting closer to and exploring this enigma—BellaRae Josephine Johnson—B.J.

Of course, I know full-well what a ridiculous name, "Pops" is—it's been haunting me all my life. Over privileged means less perspective, and my parents certainly encompassed such features. Consequently, mama and daddy thought it would be clever to purpose an old-fashioned name along-side, a tired-old pet name, in order to implant an old-soul within my unformed personality. They honestly thought this tactic would afford them less difficulty in rearing. These humbling names have assisted in keeping me less loud. Fortunately for humanity, I do not have any siblings, or at least any I claim.

In fact, to this day all my kids address me as "Pops." BellaRae has affectionately called me "Pops" ever since our first date, she only refers to me as "Bill" when she's disgusted with me. Speaking of which, I had better top off this driveway before my kids show up. Five power-house heroes, my children. Four of them I love, and one of them I tolerate. I can't wait to see them; I just need to get all this snow out of the way. But something as mindless as shoveling snow is difficult to remain focused on.

Why these are some of the biggest, crispy-clear blue-skies I've seen in years. Along with the brisk wind, it must have dumped six to eight inches of snow last night. The weather can get rather mean around here. But, so what, it is absolutely gorgeous out here, today. The blinding sun is beaming through the dancing powder-white, airborne snow-crystals effectuating multiple flashing rainbows throughout the neighborhood. Ah yes, the Morris kids are loading up their sledding gear to hit Sears Hill and try their youthful luck at the legendary "Widow-maker" ice jump. It sounds like an unforgettable thrill.

Yet, not as thrilling as my first date with BellaRae. It was August twenty-fifth, 1976 at exactly five pm when I started waiting for her in front of the admissions building. She arrived riding on a metallic-blue Fat-boy, Harley Davidson—she landed on the scene at six pm sharp. "Hey Pops, do you want a ride or are you going to stand there with your loser thumb up your loser ass, all night?" She playfully teased. Undone, I ambled over and got on her hog. I could barely greet her. As I was about to stumble over some sloppy pseudo-poetic words of welcome, B.J. abruptly stopped me with a gleaming Cheshire-cat grin, and demanded, "Wait! First close your eyes, open your mouth and stick out your tongue."

BellaRae could have insisted on anything at this moment, and I would have thought, felt, said, inhaled; eaten, killed, sucked, or fucked whatever she recommended. Without question, I opened my mouth, stuck out my tongue, but I kept one eye slightly open so I could see what she was about to do to me. She pulled a small vile of clear liquid from the inside of her bra. A dropper sealed the vile, and the label read: SANDOZ LABRATORIES; LD-25 (D-lysergic acid diethylamide). LSD. My ego screamed in terror. My mind spasmed.

Of course, I'd been curiously reading up on the documented, clinical trials and experiments with this high-powered psychedelic, executed by the likes of Dr. Humphry Osmond, Richard Alpert, and Aldous Huxley (just to name a few); because of the miraculous discovery by Dr. Albert Hofmann. Bizarrely fascinated, somewhat scared, I was halfway willing. But not altogether certain I was ready.

CHAPTER THREE
Those Wonderfully Weird Moments

"We fear our highest possibility (as well as our lowest one). We are generally afraid to become that which we can glimpse in our most perfect moments" (Abraham Maslow).

"Are you ready?" She inquired, while she hovered the dispenser of psychedelic solution a few inches above my slobbering hole of quivering lips, tongue and teeth. As BellaRae squeezed the dropper, I clenched my eyes and fists to conjure up any fortitude and courage I could to prepare myself for the proverbial mysteries of the universe to unravel before my very trivial existence. "Just breathe, Pops; it's not what you think it is," BellaRae counseled.

I opened my watery eyes after my Pilot delivered five generous drops of Hofmann's potion into my psyche; into my now altered life. Already, my perception—even more, my perspective—of BellaRae had twisted into a vision of grandiose beauty and inspiration. She became a brilliant inferno, driven by rich meaning and challenging purpose.

Just before the liquid liaison championed a submission-hold on my little world, BellaRae handed me a pink helmet to put on my soft skull, while she exposed, "I've had my eyes on you, since college. In fact, I'd dreamt about you several months before we even started our study groups, there at Suzy's pad. Anyway, tonight we ride together, and we fly together. Now get on and hold tight. I'll see you on the other side, Pops."

Clearly, on this spectacular spectacle of a night, weirdness would reign. Ruling over a kingdom of wonder, in the land of strange. On that front, just as ambivalently and impulsively as I ingested the high-powered trip-treatment, I climbed aboard her magnificent machine. BellaRae double checked to make certain I felt comfortable and secure under my pink helmet.

BellaRae gently grabbed my sweaty hands and clasped my fingers together around her voluptuous hips; she then instructed me, "Hold on tight. I ride fast and loud. Flow with the bumps and lean with me on the turns—especially the abrupt ones—so that we might maintain a sense of equilibrium, and not just mindlessly crash and burn." I could feel the L.S.D. take a deep dive as she concluded, "Enjoy the absurdity, it's all we have now."

I took a deep breath and held her closer until I could only feel her heartbeat. BellaRae's confidence soaked me with a sense of safety and security; even though she was just as anxious as I was. Her gorgeous, dark-blonde hair was braided in a tail, flying in the wind with the scent of love-potion-#9, a hint of marijuana and anticipation. She eloquently dawned a black-leather jacket, black-leather chaps, black-leather gloves (with dangling fringes), and purple leather boots.

She revved up the chariot of fire, which roared like rumbling thunder, along with an embarrassingly pleasant rattle to my nether-regions. Every gear B.J. shifted into provided a new type of euphoria. With the wind abusing my face, the scent of BellaRae in the perfect evening air, and the frenzied excitement of her supple body against mine, I felt like this was too good to be true. I almost couldn't take it, "Is this real, or just a taunting dream?" I thought.

This was just the beginning of our wonderfully weird night. For inside, I knew full-well that my life would never be the same. The sun was setting. The sky was big, blue, and beautifully saturated with translucent stars fading into their full potential. All the passing streetlights and marquees were dancing with the curious paisley and geometric shapes that would appear, then scatter, leaving behind more colors to dismantle all my vain pathologies.

Without warning, my mind went flush with my perception and perspective, descending way past my comfort-zone. When suddenly B.J. shouted, "We are almost there!" That's right, we were about to interact with this deadly public and attempt to get something to eat. The fear got a chokehold on me. I was only an hour in, on this odd odyssey when I feverishly questioned BellaRae, "When do we come down from this stuff?" In which she confidently assured me, "Oh, Pops, you'll never come down." I held her closer, and tightly closed my eyes in hopes she wouldn't notice I'd started bawling. The colorful metamorphosing visions became more vivid, more insatiable.

I was undergoing all the conflicting frequencies and vibrations of this reprocessed, moldy-cheese-laced cage we carelessly scurry about in. Frightened and bitterly scavenging for the filthy resins of all the recycled illusions we can shoot back into the veins of our unresolved lives. The cry of humanity. The "Poor me," and the "Fuck you!" BellaRae began cracking up, then I realized I was spouting this gibberish out loud.

We were riding the same wildly weird wave. And stranger yet, there was a bizarre beauty and an insightful pain within these sufferings. Because tailing this grim consciousness was an enriching comprehension, that within our core resides a valid cure for our self-imposed ills. The excellence of love. Love for ourselves and each other. We drown in the floods of disappointment and sorrow; due to the cruel abuse we impose upon ourselves, and each other. Incidentally, for no good-fucking reason at all.

It filled me with rage and compassion. Something twisted me. We were high as hell. Still, with solid resolve, we knew we were here to comfort the afflicted. This brought me to a heroic confidence, like a character in a damned-delightful book.

The irresistible awe and the painful joy this produced took me further into the profound and absurd; the likes of which I will never be blind to, again. Thousands of dancing yellow lights were flickering in perfect sync, just to the right of me. It was BellaRae's turn signal; I realized. She turned into the nearest convenient store, where she could give me some new instructions regarding the rest of our evening.

She parked the Fat-boy, put the kickstand down, and then, like a cool-breeze, got off. My liquid body refused to move from the thing; so, I sat there and starred at her with great anticipation for what's next—much like a well-trained dog waiting for a command. BellaRae looked at me for a minute with her heartbreaking, voltaic-green eyes. She then chuckled to herself as she opened the leather saddlebags draped securely over the back fender of her mean machine.

She continued by pulling a sky-blue summer dress saturated with white daises, some make-up, and a pink scarf from the durable compartment. She proceeded to explain: "Fuck the Hard Rock

Cafe. Because of the trendy stench of it, there is a high probability it is chalked full of pretentious wannabees and mindless rag dolls. We certainly do not need to wreck our wonderful ride with disappointing hype, and plastic sensationalism. But fear not, timid man, we are still going to feast. In the meantime, I need you to put this attire on and fix your plain mug up, nice and pretty. You'll fit right in. You see Pops, I am going to take you back to my dorm room where I can make you a mind-blowing meal and have you all to myself. I am certain this unexpected plan holds a refreshing element for you; especially, considering your vulnerable condition, right now." "YES!" I quickly responded.

B.J. concluded these redeeming instructions with, "So get dolled up and stay close to me." She went on into the Circle-K to check for any available lavatories, while I remained stuck to the bike twitching and chattering to myself, "How the fuck am I going to do this? Am I blowing this date?" I could see BellaRae strutting back to the entrance where she opened the door and sternly instructed me, "Let's go, Pops!" I took her good advice and forced my jelly-stricken body to seek some footing and attempt to, at least, get off this motorcycle.

As I looked up to view my progress, BellaRae was already there by my side to assist me off the two-wheeled transportation and into the next phase. She quickly took me through the colorful store, directly into the foul-smelling rest room. B.J. locked me inside the shit-stained bunker. She coached me through the door, "Get changed, Pops. I'm going to get us some gum and apple-juice. Focus, Pops! I'll be back before you fall prey to any ego melting revelations."

I found myself captive in an unexpected holding-cell, a kind of protective custody within these putrid, scum-covered walls. The overloaded toilet hadn't flushed for at least a year. It was packed full of discolored shit, decomposing in yellowish-orange fluids. The sink wasn't much better. I disrobed for the sake of our cause.

Standing on my brown corduroys, I looked past the phone numbers and scribbled obscenities covering the mirror above the clogged sink, to focus in on my wavy reflection. After a few treacherous moments when I was about to finish up, a loud and disturbing commotion jarred the strawberry-red lipstick application just outside of the bathroom door. Crash! Boom! Pow! Clang! Smack! Thunk! Bonk! Smack, smack; smack!

"Please stop, please!" I heard a man plead. Then BellaRae shouted, "Shut the fuck up, you coward! Get your rotten, bastard-ass outta' here! And I'm keeping your gun, jerk-off!" I felt like Anne Frank, quietly hiding from the doom outside. I nervously fought to slip the summer dress over my head for cover—some sort of composure. Blindly and ineffectively positioning the drape upon the rest of my body, I was stunted by the slimy bathroom door being violently kicked open. Talk about getting caught with your pants down.

Instantly, a strange sense of security calmed me when I heard B.J.'s voice utter, "Nice piece, Pops. Let me help you get this dress on. We've got to go." "What happened? Are you alright?" I asked with fear and trepidation. "Oh, it was nothing," she said, "I just had to smack an idiot's empty skull for trying to rob the place." After she appropriately placed the dress over me, BellaRae beamed in on my weary eyes, firmly gripped my shaft, and then kissed me with the passion of a couple who'd championed a lifetime of growing old together. Conquering a thug excited her.

She let loose of my lips and encouraged me, "Let's roll, handsome." B.J. guided me to the Fat-boy, while maintaining a tight grip through my dress. I was like a dog on a funky leash. A lucky dog. She helped me onto the ride and made sure that I was safely—and firmly—planted on the seat. BellaRae then straddled the driver's seat, adjusting her position until my piece perfectly enveloped between her richly rounded butt-cheeks. She fired up the soul-train and then whisked me off. Or, at least, that's how it all played-out in my psychedelic-soaked mind.

We arrived at the dorms, B.J. slowly and gracefully got off the bike. After kindly assisting me from the Harley, she briskly lifted my dress, exposing my ass so she could grab my dick from behind my thunderstruck backside. Proceeding to pull it back past my quivering nuts, she stuffed the damned thing up into my sweaty ass-crack. B.J. then informed me, "If we are going to get you into my abode, you must keep this thing tucked away."

She led me into, and up the grand stairway of the 100 plus year-old building that housed the charm of 'more honorable times', and the privacy of BellaRae's dorm room. As we were Cloak and Daggering our way through the labyrinth of these old, haunted halls, some hot blonde (wearing only a towel and way too much makeup) stopped us with an overdone smile and an over rehearsed friendly tone, which begged the question, "Hey B.J., who is your friend? Are you going to introduce us?" Judging by the disdain distorting BellaRae's facial expression, I could tell she didn't like this person. Obviously, this cheap barbie-doll's persona was nothing but more helpings of disaster at the table of decency. Without hesitation, BellaRae produced a shining smile and politely acknowledged, "Go clean your overused cunt, Nichole. Do you see any GQ-predators luring you with a flurry of objectifying attention? Now please, fuck off and mind your own useless business. Thank you." On that note, we continued with our mission.

We discreetly weaved our way through a few more of BellaRae's admirers. When at last, we reached her door. Our panic-room. Our shelter from everything and everybody else. The masks and the popular sales-pitches within the day-to-day afflictions perpetuated by dirty apes. Here is where we could nurture some uninterrupted intimacy. Some unity and solidarity, at least for now. B.J. opened her dorm-room door. Apparently, she never kept it locked. Nobody ever crossed her boundaries, because BellaRae has always made her respectful bounds clear and concise.

Her room had the delicious, mystic aroma of incense and Palo-Santos. There wasn't a single common lightbulb in the room—all differing colors, with a few brilliantly active lava-lamps. But then again, I was frying. The two single beds were covered with multiple pillows and thick comforters. She kept an endless number of books and personal writings, meticulously stacked throughout the hospitable space.

BellaRae sat me down at a small pub-table on one of the comfortable chairs. She went into her fridge to gather some grapes, strawberries, melon-slices, and apple juice (bought from the nearly robbed Circle-K) for us to replenish ourselves. She sat down with me and wondered in my eyes, as though she were examining my shadows for failures and my possibilities for greatness, while feeding me the clean fruits and the refreshing nectar. After about twenty minutes of eating, drinking, and stargazing into each other's eyes, we both succumbed to hysterical laughter. We roared ourselves into a frenzy of side splitters and perma-smile pain. I felt incredibly liberated with how secure I was in BellaRae's presence.

We ended up on the floor when B.J. stopped laughing. She tenderly put her hands on my cheeks and pulled my face to hers. Without losing eye-contact and with an unwavering confidence she stated, "I love you, Pops." BellaRae, til this very day, always says such valuable things without expecting the same words in return. I was speechless most of the ride. I may have been tripping over the edge, but I still regret not returning those words of affection.

Yet, she didn't stop there. BellaRae got up and stood above me, where she quickly disrobed. Her curves were well rounded, supple, and full in all the hottest places. BellaRae's long, muscular legs lead from her beautiful feet to her perfectly curved hips. Her pussy glistened in the reflections of the lights. With every heavy breath she took, her body quivered.

B.J. knelt over me and with her resolute hands she slowly lifted the front of my dress over the back of my head. She continued to kiss me with conviction. BellaRae put my hand on her breast, while she massaged my body in pressing, rhythmical circles. Then she took a deep breath and released an ominous moan when she found her way to my pulsating piece.

BellaRae took a firm grasp and stroked it, while her other hand continued rubbing the rest of my body. I was out of my mind. This was too much. She was in full control. So, B.J. went from kissing my neck and went down my torso, while maintaining a consistent squeeze and stroke to my obnoxious erection. The pleasure was at its boiling point as I rubbed, shook and spanked her flirting ass.

B.J. then raised my dick straight up, wildly opened her mouth and slowly hid the exited thing deep in her exotic mouth. BellaRae was sucking hard when she pressed her body to the floor and vigorously began humping it; I hung on to her ass even tighter. The deeper she could get my piece down her throat, the harder she would cum—repeatedly. After a couple of minutes of this, BellaRae stopped, sweetly looked up at me and insisted, "Don't stop."

I offered no arguments. She picked up where she left off before the unexpected command. B.J. could tell by how engorged my manic member was, that I couldn't hold back much longer. She passionately moaned and briskly began sucking harder and faster. It bolted me, "B.J. doesn't stand for BellaRae Josephine." Throughout the over-stimulation, all I could see were flashing lights; all I could hear was a loud buzz. All I could feel was too much. And then, POP! She treated it as though she was simply taking her reward, for she was the victor in charge. Because of the alien intensity of this delight, I fainted. I didn't pass-out, I fainted.

When I came to, it was morning, and BellaRae had gone. I noticed a sign pinned to the inside of her door that I didn't catch before. It read: COMFORT FOR THE AFFLICTED. Indeed, somehow, she knew her proclaimed purpose would afford her immeasurable fulfillment. With my dress still behind my head, I looked down at my naked body to observe the damage. Curiously, some sort of writing covered my chest and stomach. Moreover, it was written backwards. I stumbled over to the full-sized vanity mirror B.J. kept in the corner of her dorm room. Then I wiped the drool from the side of my mouth and the crusty sleep from my new set of eyes. And finally, focused in on the finger-painting that draped my torso, and to my welcomed surprise the sloppy opus petitioned, "Will you marry me, Pops?"

Chapter Four
Mutant Solidarity

"If I have seen further, it is by standing on the shoulders of Giants"
(Isaac Newton).

Incidentally, ten years later we married. But not under the circumstances, nor the conditions I imagined we would wed; especially considering our unconventional connection. Shortly after our matrimony we bore five high-powered paladins, the fantastic five (our inspirations); our kids, that is. In multiple ways, our children have taught us to be decent parents; and our children have compelled us throughout the years to be better people. In some unexplainable certainty, love without-condition (lots of forgiveness, to be exact) fostered us through our parent/child relationships. As it stands, our scions are our celebrated conquerors, and nothing testifies to a damned good life like the kind where you get the great honor of hanging out with your heroes.

They ought to arrive anytime now. Obviously. And everything is in its place. The driveway is almost clear. BellaRae has food and drink prepared for immediate consumption. The guest rooms (along with their amenities) are clean, organized, and ready for full-throttle exploitation. We hold an ample supply of resources for a successful Holiday-weekend, Birthday-bash. And for the next couple of days, every warm soul in our cozy home is the guest of honor. Without fail, love, gratitude, and hospitality host these celebrations every year. Make no mistake, even in the most callous weather we know how to stay warm and have some fun.

Traditionally, they all show up at the same time—and in chronological order. But I know, damned-well, they all meet Samantha at the Flying-J truck stop in Post Falls to stage the appearance of a constant coincidence. I play along though, and I always will. Because fun is a refined art. It's learned. It takes hard work and sacrifice, a steady and deep cultivation to live a good and worthwhile life.

I'd like to get out of this frigid air and warm up inside for our family's arrival. Dammit, where did I put that newspaper? Anywho, the first in line of the pseudo-convoy will be our oldest boy, Bernard. 'Berny' will attend the family gathering along with his lovely and attentive wife, Tammy. Berny and 'Tam-Tam' (as Bernard affectionately calls her) planted their roots deep in Portland, Oregon, where he is a highly respected biologist who mainly gives informative speeches to the public. He and Tam-Tam are nationally famous for their refined botany skills.

Second in line will be our youngest son, Allen. Allen has a kindhearted and incredibly smart wife, Gladys. Allen is a semi-retired Architect, because of his passion for painting his own works of art. His wife Gladys is an illustrator for graphic novels and dark (collectable) comic books. They do quite well, and those two deep thinkers will roll in from Vancouver, Washington.

In the realm of deep thinkers (as I recall) it was a few highly conscientious apostles of mind-altering art that, I think, sparked the creative and kind forces within all our children. Allen's paintings undoubtedly motivated by the amazing mural on the first wall we get to see when entering our home, which is also painted on the last wall we get to see when going back out into the callous weather. It has enriched our lives with thoughts of the greater-good. As I stand before the artistic endeavor, I understand how this genius depiction has inspired us all; especially Allen and his paintings. It's complete. It's a masterpiece. My pensive gaze staggers me as I examine every little detail.

We were fortunate enough to have this daily exhortation tattooed to the inside of our humble abode, and ultimately, to the inside of our minds. This captivating painting has the tenets for a good life nestled within the vividly colored designs, which surround the words: THOUGHTFUL, RESPECTFUL, RESPONSIBLE and FUNCTIONAL. Likewise, written just beneath this formula is a brilliant a slice of indispensable wisdom: DON'T BE 'SORRY', BE CONSIDERATE.

A team of brothers and sisters, who crafted under the business name The Grade-A Psychedelic Muzak Project executed this whole thing. They were a gentle and well-spoken crew who were difficult to procure, due to the selection process a potential client must undergo—they are quite renowned. They don't just arrive at your home and paint a conventional picture on your wall. First-off (if they select you) the eccentric group spends time with you and your family in your home, and they even cater the visits with the foods and drinks of your choice. No extra charge.

By doing this, they can get a clear sense of what is going to best edify and enrich the occupants of the awarded domicile. As it stands, The Grade-A Psychedelic Muzak Project and their influential works are a solid reward to any thriving home. And once they've collectively secured who and what your clan is about, the keen-eyed artists return the following week to engage your home with the right tone, within the right manner.

Briana, the eldest of the (artist) siblings, began revealing the endeavor by painting the fewer regrets injunction: DON'T BE 'SORRY' BE CONSIDERATE, on the lower half of our wall when exiting and the lower half of the wall when entering. Each artist knew their part—their own contribution. At the top of the painting, the second to the oldest sisters (Amber) wrote the word, Thoughtful. Next came the oldest of the brothers (Sebastian) who wrote under Amber's advice, Respectful. Right after respectful, the spot-check word Responsible initially bedaubed to the wall by the youngest brother, Donovan. And finally, at the bottom of the high-minded list, securely resting atop Briana's good council, the youngest of the siblings Veda painted the letters, Functional. The Alpha and the Omega. Full circle. Inspiring.

My family and I have profited having these words branded in our brains (consciously and innately) every day for at least the last twenty years. I am always rendered awe stricken on how this painting demonstrates just how powerfully astounding, and life altering words truly can be. That is, I have learned it is wise to recognize the frightening force of the written and spoken word. Yet, here I am again, stuck in a past only I can see—a history only I can make out. A past which seems too layered and too vast to express properly. So, it remains stuck in me, and I in it, until I am injured by the inescapable fact it will never come again.

"Damn, Pops! This mural always exacts a mysterious muse within; doesn't it?" BellaRae gently jars me back into the moment. "Absolutely gorgeous. What a magnificent masterpiece," I reply. She resumes, "Are you excited for this Holiday's capricious soiree?" "Of course, my eloquent escort. I am genuinely grateful for the continued privilege to gather with my treasured champions," I return. "Excellent," BellaRae says, "Samantha, just text me to inform us they will be here in approximately fifteen minutes. You should probably finish shoveling the driveway, right?" I raise my finger in the air as I confidently acquiesce, "Right."

Samantha, the middle child, and everything about the role of being the middle daughter embraces. She resides just a couple of towns away, in Post Falls. Samantha is a studio musician, and along with mastering drums and percussion, she lives comfortably as a music producer. And though she lives closer to us than the rest of the kids, we don't really get to see her that often. As a result of her jet-set lifestyle, she's never married or had any children of her own. Samantha deeply loves her family and takes great honor and joy in these Holiday visits. Or, at least, appears as though she feels like she has fulfilled her annual obligation.

Which brings us to our second-to-the-youngest daughter, Dianna. Dianna is married to a fine gentleman who goes by the name of Seth; Seth owns his own car dealership. Dianna is the proprietress and operator of a lucrative marijuana grow-farm, which produces high (emphasis on high) quality distillates, oils and edibles of all sorts. The title of her company is Melting Pot Extracts. Her and Seth live in Spokane, Washington, where Dianna is known for being a bit of a psychedelic/entheogen guru. And just for shits and giggles, Dianna and Seth rebuild old motorcycles—mainly vintage Harleys. I can't wait to smell the tasty flowers she'll be bringing to our family shindig.

Last, and loud, is our youngest daughter, Mercy. We carefully picked the children's names; no other name was as reflective to BellaRae and I than this one. Mercy is a sought-out singer/songwriter, and a professional piano player. She's also an insightful columnist for a high-profile music magazine. Much like the rest of her siblings, Mercy naturally enjoys keeping her heart, mind and soul vigilant and resolute with enriching occupations.

BellaRae and I hail ourselves all too fortunate with the good company of our delightful descendants, who have evolved into sophisticated and decent individuals. Because as a psychologist, I know full well not all parents and/or children arrive in life with the same value advantages. The things I've seen and heard as a psychologist will still somehow strike me down into a grim and foul mood.

"They are here!" BellaRae gleefully cheers as she runs out the front door to greet our valued loved ones. I get tearful with an overwhelming gratitude in these precious moments. Meanwhile, my family must park their cars out on the road because I still haven't finished shoveling the damned driveway. I also need to contact the paperboy again; I haven't been able to find today's newspaper yet. For now, I will greet my kids and bring their luggage in doors; then I will finish the driveway. I love this time of year for just one reason, family.

As we get inside and close the door behind us, we exchange hugs and hellos. We then admire and comment on the mural. Yet, without welcome and over our chatter, I hear Pink Floyd blaring down the street, and it's creeping closer and closer to our sanctuary. "Son-of-a-bitch! It's him!" I urgently yelp, while I sprint out the front door to the half-shoveled driveway.

CHAPTER FIVE
Easy Writer

"...and every day, the paperboy brings more" (Pink Floyd).

In reaching the driveway, I finally see the newspaper delivered earlier this morning. I'm standing directly over it right now. It's a treacherous disservice I constantly dump upon Solomon, our paperboy; the foul-mouthed, rotten bastard he is. He's some sort of self-aggrandized version of a low-budget, sideshow freak. He's a bizarre distraction from the wreckage we leave behind and the shadows that 'boo' us, therein. However, I'm the one who will look like an imbecile once again. Dammit, he's practically here.

Unfortunately, twice a week, even more so around the Holidays I become a bit distracted by my own mental masturbation and overlook the morning newspaper. Which he delivers daily, without fail, before I get up. Consequently, I call the main office and complain, "Where's my goddamned paper?!" As a result, Solomon (our fifty-year-old paperboy) receives a call by his directors who remind him he is under contract and must out of his way and deliver another newspaper to me. One could say through the years Solomon and I have fostered a brutal and monstrous camaraderie.

Driving up, he makes direct eye-contact, and I fall prey to his condescending grin. However, like a shining paragon, Mrs. Hyneezitzs brazenly struts down from the house to the setting at hand. She obviously heard the loud music creeping through our quiet neighborhood. In her tricky right hand, she waves a classy five-hundred-dollar bill high enough in the barbarous air for our daily deliverer to note, while maintaining Solomon in her sights. As she passes me to take her position, she quietly jeers, "Again, Bill? I can save your ass this time, just not your face." Our loved ones gather at the front window to spectate the moron (me), being made a fool of.

And here is the nasty, irritating itch about this alien in a stranger's body—our paperboy, Solomon. My wife finds the crazed courier a bit too likeable if you ask me. She professes he's a cross between a quirky nightmare, and a dream come true. Every episode with this guy is deeply discrediting.

BellaRae poses three feet to my left. Solomon pulls into the driveway, and respectfully parks his car directly in front of me. With an unrelenting, sinister stare, he politely opens his car door and steps out into the chill to deal with me in a "civilized" fashion. His broad-shouldered, five-foot eleven body maneuvers out of the compact car with an unexpected agility much like his word choices. That's right, he hails himself a writer—whatever.

With a sense of urgency to his long footing, Solomon jauntily lumbers toward me with a freshly rolled newspaper in his hand. Wearing nothing but pink Bermuda-shorts, unlaced snow-boots, and a dark-purple scarf dangling over a black T-shirt that reads, "I LOVE BANGKOK," in neon-red letters. Big, weird hands, lost-in-space eyes, neatly groomed blonde hair and graying-goatee; Solomon is potent. I can't fucking stand him.

Immediately, and without a hint of thoughtful hesitation, I stumble over the same tired-old wordy excuses. And Solomon, with a deranged, million-dollar smile and a galaxy in his stoned eyes, heckles, "Stick a dick in it, Doc.; here's your other paper." He generously hands me the fresh paper, as I explain, "Yeah, I've been shoveling the damned driveway all morning, while looking for today's paper; I've been out here all morning and still no sign of it. Believe me, Solomon, nothing." He looks specifically at the paper I've been foolishly failing to hide under my new boots and a dirty chunk of frozen snow remarks, "I believe everything, and trust nobody. One thing I can always count on is self-interest."

BellaRae rushes over to us, smiling pleasantly at Solomon. Solomon's girlfriend still in the warm car watches Mrs. Hyneezitzs with a hawkish stare. My wife gestures the big tip to the overpaid paper-slinger resolving, "You have more than earned this; please accept our meager gift for your excellent services." She ardently grabs his over-worked right hand with both of hers and warmly places the currency within his grateful grip. With a cheerful grin, a sly wink, and a bedroom tone, Solomon counters, "Thank you, and Merry Christmas." Slowly, he slips the spoils from her friendly hands. I fucking despise him.

As it stands, in all my years of psychology I have observed without fail nobody, no matter how wonderful (no matter how beautiful inside and out) can compete with the wily lures of infatuation. Solomon turns back to me and rants, "Your reoccurring antics have sliced into my busy day, sir. Not to mention, I've been up all night throwing bad news at the doorways of assholes, megalomaniacs, and jags. And my breath reeks like I've been eating ass all night." Simultaneously, his voluptuous girlfriend and my wife raise their eyebrows with an applauding, "Mmmmmmm... sounds good."

Desperately attempting to distract them from this socially unacceptable buzz, I ask Solomon when was the last he had been to Bangkok. In which he nefariously suggests, "Bangkok is a place?" The self-monikered 'writer' continues on to philosophy, "Why labor over your arguments, Doc. when you can develop your story? I know damn-well you're hoarding a mountain of maniacal memoirs you've stashed away in that menacing mind of yours." My thoughts race, stagger and buckle for some form of composer. No matter how feeble and depraved.

Impulsively, I reach for some low-hanging fruit with, "So, what are you writing about these days, Solomon?" I force-feed a face of sincere fascination. He shuts his big mouth, strokes his goatee, looks down at the ground (directly where I am standing on today's paper) and then he laughs to himself. It only takes a slight spark in his eye for him to look up again and examine me. Make no mistake, it felt like I'd finally jolted him. For one glorious moment, I was pretentiously reading this cheap contradiction like a poorly written comic strip. What a narcissistic fool, I think to myself. What a hideous reflection.

With infiltrating eye correspondence and a cocky 'shame be damned' tone the vulgar author concludes, "You, sukkah." On this note, Solomon opens his car door, casually gets into his car and gently closes his door. He and his pretty partner blow kisses and smiles to us as they slowly drive away. Driving off, Solomon opens his window, raises his fist in the stiff air and roars, "In your head, sukkah!" In which I no longer see his girlfriend's, for that matter.

BellaRae and I inspect the work remaining in shoveling this damned driveway. I step off the chunk of dirty snow, which was supposed to be covering the newspaper, and regardless of my new boots, I slip and fall. Thankfully, I land in a part of the driveway where I have not tended to it yet. The back of my coat gets chalked full of frigid snow, not a graceful landing. But no irreparable harm has been done. B.J. (my wife) helps me up and pulls me into her warm, welcoming body. She plants a passionate kiss on my foot-flavored lips. She's forgiving, she's merciful towards me.

She's always there to help me up when I fall. She always helps me find my way back to the right track, and I need it. We need it. I get stuck in my mind with resentments of shattered ideals in which I thought I was smart enough to materialize. One of many penalties I've achieved with the arrogance of my own successes. As a result, I miss out on the good life which unfolds before me (mostly unnoticed) every day. I'm medically retired because I'm not altogether well.

In fact, midway through my career I suffered a mental and emotional breakdown, because of a savage case I pridefully fought to undertake by myself. I was showing off, but it was a viciously painful case; one which dropped me into the dark depth of taunting trepidation. This involved a family of great tragedy: Clark Williams (the dad), Vanity Williams (Clark's wife), and their two children Grace (the eldest sibling) and the youngest, David. I seem to refuse to let go of the heartache and the mental anguish regarding the brutal William's case.

My obsessive mind takes my thoughts hostage, meanwhile I overlook my good life. I'm doing much better, because of BellaRae's help and understanding. Thanks to her, I've come a long way. We named our youngest daughter Mercy, so would not forget where I came from; how far I had fallen. Never do I want to fall that far again.

At any rate, I see my kids chuckling at me after my interaction with Solomon. BellaRae goes back inside with reasonable hopes of me topping off this driveway. While I shovel, I can barely concentrate and keep my thoughts from being saturated with Solomon and what I should have said to him. But without notice, my mind becomes besieged by the torment of the William's case.

CHAPTER SIX
Grace

*"We shall describe conditions of the soul that words can only hint at.
We shall have to use logic to try to corner perspectives that laugh at
our attempt"* (Huston Smith).

Unmercifully, four things come to mind every time I remember Grace Williams. Her and her tragic family. Grace clung to a solid and reasonable sense of right and wrong, which generated her resolute and rigorous honesty (the only language she spoke fluently). Her name held validity within the generous character Grace distributed to anybody she came face-to-face with. The suffering such a person had to abide, moves me into a vigorous resentment towards humanity. Grace Williams was the first patient I interviewed and evaluated, after I'd thoroughly reviewed the police reports, confessions, medical records and the autopsy.

It was 1981, and I had recently topped-off my internship under Dr. Humphry Osmond in Saskatchewan, at the Weyburn Psychiatric Hospital where I learned the indisputable truth: "With much wisdom comes much sorrow, the more knowledge the more grief." And the fact is, even in times of joy, happiness, and celebration there remains a baseline of sadness ever omnipresent. I rapidly landed the beginnings of a solid career at Creedmoor Psychiatric Center in Queens Village, Queens, New York.

Or, at least, so I had thought. I was pretentiously moving forward in my profession on the vexing edge of confidence and cockiness. But I soon discovered even a highly schooled, well-trained doctor offers no significant solutions when presumption dictates the diagnosis. Only well-seasoned physicians hold the wisdom and integrity to heal—to comfort the afflicted. Impatiently tenacious as I was (ready to get the world by the nuts) they assigned me my first full-force case load. It was legendary at Creedmoor because it was one of the most arduous cases to come through the Center's doors (I, in retrospect, was completely unequipped for this life-changing assignment). The William's Case.

It was utterly ostentatious for me (or anybody else) to think I could handle a load of this caliber—carry this weight. And those who worked alongside me were eager to see if I could 'handle it' without becoming a patient at Creedmoor, myself. In fact, my own pretentious views of my abilities drove me to push for the most troublesome cases; and my arrogance briskly found the treachery it was looking for.

This file comprised a toddler named David, a young girl, Grace (David's sister) their mother, Vanity, and Clark, Grace and David's dad. Vanity, Grace's mother, worked part time as a waitress, yet she always bragged to others how she was a stay-at-home mom who constantly "tended to the household duties and the children". Clark (Grace and David's dad) worked long, hard hours to provide for his family, which meant Vanity didn't need to work. Vanity would protest to Clark she needed the break from the kids. However, the truth is she used work as a disguise in order to foster her nasty addictions to alcohol, cocaine, and lowbrow scumbags who had no respect for the sanctity of family.

Absurdly enough, Vanity took the children to church every Wednesday and Sunday. Mainly because her pastor wasn't just her drug dealer, but he was also one of her lovers. They got together one of the many times Vanity was trying to 'get her shit together'. Yet, worst of all, because of her hatred and fear towards men, she would take her demons out on poor little David (beat the shit out of him) for any inconvenience he would cause her. In other words, any normal child behavior was typically exasperating to Vanity. Whenever Grace would attempt to intervene, she would get beat as well, a preponderance of the time to the point of unconsciousness. Ultimately, Grace and David were beat-up a fist-full of times, which is a hideous disgrace even for a drunken coke-whore. Grace and David were eventually liberated from the tyranny of these horrors. Just not the nightmares.

Other times, Vanity would simply block David out by keeping him secluded in the basement, while Grace took care of the household chores. Grace would wait for Vanity to get inebriated and pass-out (which never took long) she would then sneak down to the basement to care for, play with and comfort her little brother. Every day, Vanity kept an alarm set to go off an hour before Clark was due to be home, so she could get everybody in their places to appear "normal".

Clark worked twelve-hour days, five to six days a week, as a truck mechanic. Unfortunately, his job required him to work out of town a few weeks out of the year. The heavier beatings typically occurred on those occasions when Clark had to work a week or two away from home. Anytime a bruise needed explanation (or a broken bone, chipped tooth, timid affect, stitches, etc.), regarding Grace and/or David, Vanity would blame the child with an accidental 'fall down the stairs', 'tumbling off a chair', or even a 'bicycle injury'. "Kids will be kids, Clark," Vanity (with a shrug of her shoulder) would carelessly conclude.

Grace and David always felt safe (relieved really) when their Dad was home; according to them, they were genuinely happy when Clark was around because he made them feel secure. He made them feel as if everything would be alright. Grace was always apprehensive to inform Clark of Vanity's cruelties, because of the looming threats of the punishments becoming harsher, colder; Vanity was noticeably clear on this front. Grace loved her mother. She pitied her, and yet, Grace knew full well Vanity's threats would be rare promises she would fulfill.

Grace took care of everything, even to the point of missing school from time to time, while her dad was gone at work: David, the household duties, the meals, the yard, and even her mother. Vanity could remain drunk on denial, and high on oblivion. Grace loathed her mother's vicious outbursts and evil ways. Still, she held a bit of compassion for Vanity. Grace felt sorry for Vanity and the burdens she gloried in, a tormented mind, a callous heart, and her mangled soul. Somehow, Grace knew her mother hated her own heartless deeds and her frigid reactions towards life. Vanity reviled her own existence; she despised her own survival.

Clark, on the other hand, found great purpose and meaning in being a dad. His convictions drove him to put in the long hard hours of work, which in his mind would assure his children a better life. Clark's limited hours spent at home were typically absorbed in his children, while trying to keep the peace within Vanity's sporadic mood swings. Clark wasn't necessarily a saint, but the authentic love for his children and the vision he believed his family could achieve; continuously inspired him to be a better person for his friends, and especially his family. As far as Clark was concerned, being a Dad altered him in optimistic ways.

But all these noble illusions were shattered for the Williams family, August seventeenth, nineteen hundred and eighty. Little David was well into his threes, Grace was sixteen. Clark was getting home unusually early from a job he was, originally, supposed to be out of town for "approximately" another week. Incidentally, he didn't inform his wife nor his children of his premature arrival, because of the surprise trip to Knott's Berry's Farm and Disneyland he had secretly planned for them months in advance.

Meanwhile, Vanity had been drinking, drugging, and wallowing in bitterness throughout the night, only to spin out into this terrible day. Grace had been anxiously attempting to cover all the household responsibilities; not to mention, keeping David clear of their mother's increasingly hostile darkness. Grace could hear her mother bickering with herself, through the ghastly hours of the night before. More drinks, more drugs, more hatred.

Also, just being dumped for somebody better looking, dumber and more reckless by her most recent lover, didn't help Vanity's nasty disposition. Vanity's pastor (whom she caught in a morbidly compromised position with, yet another member of the congregation) also happened to be her drug dealer. Reverend Grope was very generous with his addictions, especially with the lonely and not so stable homemakers of his church. Even worse, in this grim hour, Vanity was on her last line of coke. She was three bottles-deep on cheap wine, along with multiple shots of Southern Comfort and heavy doses of resentment.

The pending doom became titanic. Sometimes Grace's saving grace was the fact Vanity favored Grace, and Grace felt guilty because of it; still, Vanity loathed each family member equally when she was drunk. And though Vanity blamed her family for all her woes, Grace could maneuver around Vanity's vile views unlike anybody else. Grace used this shaky ground to keep her brother as safe as she could.

Twelve forty-five pm, approximately one hour since Vanity took her last line of coke and she remains unwilling to admit defeat and crash. Grace was keeping David in the kitchen beside her, while she washed the breakfast dishes in preparation for making lunch. Normally, Grace would keep David close to her side and out of the firing line of Vanity's demonic rage. Grace could sense the menacing tension running amok, though. She knew she and David were in danger.

Vanity had just topped off her last bottle of wine. She then staggered into the kitchen where Grace was finishing the dishes, while David played with his Play-Doh three feet away from his sister. Vanity lost her balance and fell into the breakfast bar, losing control of her empty bottle, which loudly shattered into shards of broken glass all over the kitchen floor. The bracing crash frightened everybody in the room, especially little David who screamed when one of those sharp shards imbedded itself into his right forearm; never mind the abrupt halt to the little peace Grace and David were attempting to savor. Unfortunately, the child's cry for help—the sounds of responsibility—jarred Vanity too far out of her depraved comforts and locked her into the throes of a ferocious stupor.

"Shut up!" Vanity screamed at David. "I'll give you something to cry about, you piece of shit!" Vanity lunged toward David (who was already bleeding, scared and crying) with her typical satanic look searing through her washed-out eyes. "Mama, please no!" Grace pleaded. Grace just simply couldn't bare another brutal beating upon her defenseless brother. She pulled her mother away from David's direction by Vanity's favorite blouse (Vanity always said it was the most flattering shirt she owned), which tore in the intervention. Stunned, Vanity scrambled to gather some steady footing against the kitchen counter, where she got ahold of a freshly hand cleaned steak-knife and impulsively stuck it in Grace's right thigh.

Meanwhile, Clark just parked the car in the driveway and was getting out of the vehicle when he heard Grace scream with great terror and disorienting distress. "No! No! Please! Stop!" Until this moment Clark never heard Grace scream, much less in this manner. All six-foot-six, two hundred and ninety pounds of Clark's frame charged for the front door (which led directly into the kitchen), like an angry bull looking to crush an enemy underfoot. Unfortunately, before he could get to, and through the door, Vanity was able to get back to her original target of resentment—little David.

Like a fiendish sadist, Vanity backhanded her youngest child, which threw him backward, causing little David to hit the back of his head squarely on the unwavering tile floor. He was knocked unconscious on impact, sending him into a full-blown seizure. Vanity's megalomania clouded her perception so deeply, she didn't even recognize her son's compromised condition. She clenched her right hand into an angry fist, which she quickly cocked back to fire upon her prey. "You selfish, fucking bastard!" Vanity bemoaned, as she landed a malicious blow directly in the middle of David's vulnerable face.

In a moment, Clark threw open the kitchen door. Instantly, all illusions of his offspring's past wounds being accidental were subdued with fierce reality. "Daddy!" Grace shouted with monumental relief and restless anguish. Vanity had her bitter fist raised for another landing on the baby's skull. But the crash of the kitchen door and Grace's proclamation of rescue interrupted Vanity, who turned towards the children's proud Father with the frightful look of a rodent scurrying back into the darkness, after a light suddenly switched on.

Stone-cold sober, Vanity rose to her feet and swiftly inquired, "Clark?" Clark could only see his son convulsing, his little boy's arms stiff in the air and his legs rattling against the floor like boards. His pain and rage escalated when he also witnessed his daughter bleeding profusely (after she just pulled the weapon from her leg); Grace labored to get to David's aid. She kept a dish towel compressed against the knife wound to retard the bleeding.

Clark's hopes and dreams, his meaning and purpose, lie utterly broken and bleeding all over the kitchen floor. All of which were now irreparable pieces. It only took a second for him to regain his breath and make his next move; one last, final decision. The sessions I encountered with the William's family put me in such a state, where countless times I would reach for reminders to just simply breathe, while each revelation of the incident slowly tore away at my faculties.

Dr. Hyneezitzs: "Okay Grace, you are doing very well. Just breathe...If you are able, would you please describe to me what happened next?"

Grace: "Yes, of course, doctor. Are you alright?"

Dr. Hyneezitzs: "Of course, I'm here for you. Please, continue."

Grace: "Well, at first, my dad's face had the look of bottomless sorrow, unforgiving regret, and bitter disillusionment. As his tears increased, so did his breathing; his face turned blood red. The second he looked Vanity dead in the eyes and witnessed the demons she had been fostering, his eyes became a consuming fire.

My Dad went on and calmly instructed me (without losing sight of Vanity's trembling position) 'Grace, please call 911 and comfort David.' Vanity winced in a desperate voice asking, 'Clark?' As he slowly cornered her like a hungry butcher about to slaughter a fattened pig."

Dr. Hyneezitzs: "At this point, what was going through your mind, Grace?"

Grace: "My head was mostly spinning, but I could somehow call emergency and tend to David as quickly as possible. I also thought how grateful I am Dad is home"

Dr. Hyneezitzs: "Did you know what was going to happen next?"

Grace: "Absolutely, Doc. But please understand, I loved my mother very much. It was simply time. I mean, enough was enough."

Dr. Hyneezitzs: "Time for what?"

Grace: "As my dad wrapped both of his enraged, hard-working hands securely around her hicky infested neck; there was no resistance nor hesitation from either of them, 'at this point'—as you inquired. It was as if their lives were meant for this moment, and both had succumbed to their purpose. My dad's forearms turned purple as he bore down on her jugulars; the more the veins in his arms popped, the more the vessels in Vanity's face popped. It appeared to be the first sincere connection they'd had with each other, in a very long time. I embraced David, wiping away his blood, checking his breathing, and whispering in his ear, 'everything is going to be alright little buddy, just breathe'. Meanwhile, my eyes never left my mother and father's last interaction. Her eyes bulged and bled as my dad constricted his hands tighter around her failing neck. I heard her capillaries and bones crack, snap and burst, while her body shook limp. It was completely silent when the gloom and murk my mother carried with her everywhere, suddenly dissipated and left the room. However, a different darkness haunted us then."

Dr. Hyneezitzs: "What darkness are you speaking of?"

Grace: "Grief...My Dad let go, dropping the corpse to the floor. My dad then fell to his knees and crawled to David and me; my bleeding was under control with the compression of the towel. Just before my Dad's tears overtook him, he asked me a second time to call for help. He held David close as he wept profoundly. After calling the proper authorities, I sat with Dad and David embracing each other while we mourned; until the police and the paramedics arrived. Since then, I haven't gotten to hug my Dad in a year." Grace wept. "Unlike the other kids in school, I'll never get the chance to take my parents for granted," she realized through her terrible tears.

Grace and David were improving reasonably well since Vanity's passing, so I closed the session with the resolve of never mentioning her, again. "Thank you, Grace," I concluded. "You did exceptionally well, today. I'll continue to push for a supervised visit with your Dad. Maybe the courts will show some mercy with the holidays coming up."

Grace: "Thank you, Doctor. It would mean the world to David and me."

CHAPTER SEVEN
Vanity

"But the way of the wicked is like deep darkness; they do not know what makes them stumble" (Proverbs 4:19).

"Check it out, Pops," BellaRae distracts. "The Morris family are arriving home later than usual tonight," she continues, "Judging by the cast plastered around the oldest (Casey Morris) boy's right arm, he must have tried his bad luck with the legendary 'Widow-Maker'." I vicariously perked up to see. Sure enough, Casey broke his damned arm sledding off the old Widow-Maker. How fucking exciting! Just to do something so recklessly exhilarating; Casey Morris is simply fearless, wow. "Wow, what an idiot," BellaRae declares.

With zero hesitation and clumsy urgency, everybody in the room beelines it to the main window, which is now open viewing to today's moron—the modern-day clown. Like a bunch of imbeciles, we all gather to gaze upon the fool. Yet, we don't just observe for morbid fascination and curious mockery. On the contrary, we want to see what led this person (or persons) to such a disastrous decision; and how they are coping with those impulsive behaviors, now. Obviously, so we might never enjoy the same kinds of regretful broken trophies. So we don't turn away. We take note. We learn.

During my college years, I had a philosophy Professor who gave our idealistic-minds this scenario to gnaw on; whereby one may live in this utopian town/society which supplies folks with all their needs, and even all their wants. If it's a perfect family one desires, their family's needs and wants would also be provided for.

The only requirement for this arrangement (in such a crowd) is to observe, for only 45 minutes a day, an isolated, scared and unloved child. The only cost. All one would have to do to live in, and with such a society is watch this one child suffer once a day. The Vanity I met would have no remorse—and no second thoughts—with such a contract.

I wonder though, is it cruel to watch somebody struggle without some sort of intervention? Even if it's a chump who is accustomed to and irrationally addicted to failure? Such a person, indeed, would take no issue in watching another suffer, and perhaps solely for the luxurious sake of laziness. Sins of omission. Possibly take a twisted pleasure in such things. These creatures are alive and resentful about it. Such is the odious, reoccurring-recollection, concerning the first time I encountered Vanity.

It was during my internship under Dr. Humphry Osmond, in the beautiful land of Saskatchewan at the Weyburn Psychiatric Hospital between the strange and sensational years of 1978, and seventy-nine. Vanity was legally admitted, specifically and especially, to Weyburn for Dr. Osmond's successful expertise and therapies. His unique and vast insights into the demented labyrinth (our beast-of-burden) the human mind was invaluable. Particularly with disturbed minds like Vanity's.

Vanity was court-ordered into Weyburn, in order to get her shit together again, but this time for her family's safety. She had been to jails and mental institutions multiple times for drug abuse, alcohol abuse, and nervous breakdowns ever since she was a young teen. Years before Vanity met and married Clark, she set fire to her mother's house (with her mother still sleeping inside) one callous Christmas morning. Her mother barely escaped the flames and remained terrified of Vanity until the day she died (her mother died five years before Vanity had Grace). It took seven police-officers to subdue Vanity at the crime scene, while she was having her 'fit'. She claimed she was just angry and got too drunk. She pled temporary insanity to the courts (temporary, my ass). Vanity was sixteen at the time.

This time, however, Vanity's mental breakdown was because of a heinous case of post-partum depression. She had recently given birth to her second child, David. Vanity's daughter Grace was fourteen during this admission. Clark, Vanity's weary husband, was supportive yet concerned for his children's safety. Clark felt she was drinking too much, too soon after David's birth. And the last time he approached her about it, she became uncontrollably violent. Even towards her children. Clark gathered enough testimonial of her over all shit-show to have her, at a minimum, evaluated. Which, of course, required her to be committed against her will.

Meanwhile, I was to follow Dr. Osmond's evaluations, analysis and therapies, regarding his patients. This included Vanity's court-ordered case. Unfortunately, she required chemical restraint through-out her entire stay (or hold) in Weyburn. In fact, most of her early sessions required physical restraints. It seemed as if every time she spoke, her own words would escalate her psychotic hostilities towards anybody who was listening, or just in proximity.

Because of her resistance, Dr. Osmond could not exact his careful usage of psychedelics on Vanity's troublesome issues, due to the sedatives she had to be under. Besides, Dr. Osmond perceived her ills to be much more deeply rooted than psychological. He told me in confidence—off the record—Vanity had voluntarily mangled her own soul.

Vanity was a terrible concern. I, too, held significant fears for her children's well-being, particularly if the kids were to be left in the lurch of her "care". Nevertheless, I had no say, I had no credentials and absolutely no control over the outcome of the court's decisions. Nobody did. The courts were too bogged down for these sensitive matters; the judge had no legitimate understanding of Vanity's unstable condition. And the worst the magistrate could do would be to release Vanity back over to her family.

Yet, amid her cryptic song-n-dance and volatile outbursts, Dr. Osmond was working diligently to dissect enough of her charade to discern what the root-cause of her morbid darkness might be. And from his observations and within my pupil perspective, it wasn't Vanity's insanity that scared us so much; it was her solutions we found hazardous.

She was fostering some deeply nefarious resentments. Vanity grew up without a father, or at least one who would claim her. Her mother was a pill-popping, drunken mess. Vanity's mom never thought of her as more than an accident who ruined her life, and she hated Vanity for it. In other words, not only was Vanity unwanted by her mother, but her mother also remained dangerously neglectful of her throughout her most vulnerable years. Vanity's mother's addictions came first, which took all her time and attention away from little Vanity.

Time away from young Vanity's nurturing, safety and well-being. Attention away from the disturbing damage her male callers were imposing on Vanity, which strongly contributed to Vanity's beliefs in humanity. All the experts concluded, in part, Vanity's grim childhood molded her into the tough case she had become. A vexing of the spirit. Simply put, nothing more than a drain on resources. At least, judging by court decisions.

According to my calculations whilst observing Vanity's defence-mechanisms, manipulations, and subtle deceptions; she had an unrelenting way of breaking a person down. Still, Vanity taught me one valuable truth; the most cunning and arduous thing about resolve is the resistance. Make no mistake, Vanity shamelessly resisted most anything reasonable, practical, or just plain decent. But the day came when she slipped and accidently spoke honestly.

She started forgetting which mask she was wearing. "I could feel good and accepted for a few minutes, or I could feel shame and rejection for a life-time," Vanity randomly blurted-out during one of our last sessions with her. During some of her other emotional and mental breakdowns, Vanity would uncontrollably spill-out some sort of conscious candor. Just when she was about to be released back into the custody of the state, we finally scored a lottery-winning moment. All the difficult laboring payed-off; the precious jewel of comprehension. But only for a moment.

Disappointingly, we had very little time to treat Vanity, because of her pastor persuading the judge in charge of Vanity's case. This pastor was very clever. Somehow, he was able to convince the judge it would be in his and the communities' best interest to release her early (against medical advice) with the condition she regularly attend church, and the counseling services provided by said church. Politics and religion, charm and beauty stole the win on this one.

"My father never claimed me. I never knew him; he was never in my life—motherfucker!" Vanity ranted. She continued, "My mother was never present. She never really cared enough to pay any real attention to me. My mother was devoted to drugs, drinking, and losers. Idiots who didn't bother figuring out how to do life and didn't bother thinking-twice about doing a minor." Dr. Osmond inquired, "Your mother never knew, she didn't intervene?"

Vanity revealed, "The one time I reluctantly went to her for help, because one of her many loser boyfriends was raping me; she reacted by beating me to a bloody-mess. After the beating, she spit on me and screamed, 'How dare you!' She then left for the night. I was only seven years old."

Dr. Osmond peeled back the next layer, "And none of these sick bastards ever took 'no' for an answer?" Vanity's throat-cutting reply was, "After my mother's reaction, I made a promise to myself to never say no, again. Men are worthless and weak scumbags. They're easy to play; they do everything in vain. And women aren't any better."

"Alright, Pops, focus. We've got to get going, immediately. Our family is hungry, and you are making us late for our reservation. We also need to stop and get the poor stupid Morris boy a GET WELL SOON gift. We'll drop it by tomorrow, before our Christmas-Eve dinner. Now let's go, sukkah!" BellaRae has always had a remarkable way of keeping things on the right track. She's always been able to bring me into the present moment, where I can take a deep sigh of relief. A breath of fresh air.

CHAPTER EIGHT
The Preacher

"He was lame from his hurts, and the weight bent him double. Yet even so, inch by inch, still availing himself every scrap of cover, he set out on his Via Dolorosa to the bus, carrying his torture" (C. S. Lewis).

"It's becoming ridiculously clear to me; we really should start putting Casey Morris on our Christmas list. The knuckle-head gets himself hurt every damned year," BellaRae strains. "No shit," Adam and Mercy chime in. Samantha, cranky from hunger, interrupts, "Stop, already! The server is coming, and we need to order before this develops into, yet another useless story." Her siblings oblige (always keeping things in good humor), "No shit!" they loosely say. We share a quick and quiet chuckle amongst ourselves.

It's irrational why I do it, but I always order the crab or lobster; even though we always have a crab and lobster dinner every Christmas-eve. "Bill, if you get the lobster or the crab, I'll rip the three last strands of hair out, you use to comb over your nervous skull," BellaRae threatens, clearly and quietly in my twitching ear.

Alas, the server. He's tanned, his hair and beard are heavily groomed, and his rehearsed smile is even more fake than his tan. He politely asks, "What might I get you good-folks, tonight?"

Performing his task with striking precision. I lean over to my wife and whisper, "What a fake. I could penetrate his little disguise in one session, and in the end have him whaling for his mama's tit." Without her eyes leaving the perfect physique of our server, BellaRae whispers back, "I think he's cute...Let's order, now."

Everybody orders the spareribs, I, on the other hand, order the lobster. BellaRae stomps on my tiny toe with the heel of her stiletto boot, while giving a playful smile and wink to the haughty server. I still get my lobster. The handsomely eloquent hustle the server demonstrates for a tip, gets me thinking of the preacher. Pastor Grope. The preacher who gave a charmingly persuasive pitch to the judge in order to have Vanity released from therapy way too soon. Therapy Vanity desperately needed. He was one of the last people to know her intimately. Not just because he was her drug dealer, but he was also her last lover. They had quite a torrid affair.

It was a part of my duty to retrieve any information I could from Pastor Grope regarding the William's incident. The courts believed it would add more context to what they should do with the nasty death-penalty hanging over Clark's head. And whether Grace and David could ever see their Dad, again. Pastor Arlee Austin Grope was indeed charming, good-looking, and exhaustively sly.

He didn't arrive willingly, though; he had to be subpoenaed for this psychological interview. The preacher strutted in with an enormous smile and dressed to kill. He gave me a firm handshake and made himself comfortable on the patient couch. With a jolly tone he humored me, "What can I do for you today, Sir?" He reeked of cologne, cigarettes and other poor decisions. He wasn't fooling me, but it didn't stop him from trying. Even he knew I wasn't blind to his shortcomings, but the sick cycle of addiction is the addict is fully devoted to the cycle. However, I wondered if he knew anything about Vanity the rest of us didn't?

She attended his church for seven years. Also, the preacher married Vanity and Clark; Pastor Grope even baptized their children. While the William's kids were in Grope's daycare (and while Clark was at work), he was snorting coke in his office with Vanity. He always hung a sign outside of his office door during these occasions to detour passers-by: DO NOT DISTURB! COUNSELING IN SESSION. Nice. And in like manner, he was high-as-hell for our session, as well.

"Mr. Grope, as you know, the court ordered you here so that we might learn what you know about Clark, Vanity, Grace and David. More specifically, Vanity. This is so we might study more thoroughly, what may have contributed to the drugs, the abuse, and the incident regarding Vanity's death," I presented to the preacher.

"What the hell? She was mother-fucking killed," the preacher proclaimed. "Yeah, that's right, I know you had the judge force me here to do this jive-ass bullshit. I didn't really know that poor bastard, or his kids. And yeah, I may have supplied his freaky bitch dope and fucked her a few times; but I never paid no attention to Grace and David. Hell, I haven't got no time for my own kids. Shit, Vanity's kids never seemed to matter to her much, anyway. All she cared about was getting wasted and getting used. I've been slinging dope since I was little. You should know damn well Doc, denial may be our drug of choice, but it's our own defiance that keeps us high. But the facts don't rid me of this looming guilt; it never seems to go away."

After pulling out a flask of whiskey from the inside pocket of his very expensive suit, in which he could obsessively sip on while he ranted, "I might drink too much," the preacher continued, "I might drug too much, and use white bitches; but I'm a pillar in this community. I know damned-well it isn't right. None of it. But it's the eighties, and these are the end times. I am finally winning at the game. Eating cheese at the rat race. I know I've got to get right with God. Like a fool, I chase illusions of happiness and still disappointed by the hand-full after hand-full of emptiness it offers every damned time. Just like Vanity, she offered nothing good to anybody.

I never asked her many questions, Doc. Any woman I ever had an affair with was nothing but damaged goods. I mean, digging for answers from a liar allows no certainty, and certainly no fucking satisfaction. So, I never jumped into any 'how was your day' type of bullshit with her. But make no mistake, that wicked bitch was crazy. She sucked and fucked like she was possessed, and she kept the gas tank of my brand-new Cadillac full from all the dope she snorted. I can honestly testify; I've seen lipstick on a pig.

I know it wasn't right to have that evil cunt released from you experts, knowing damned well she needed the help. I feel bad for Clark and his kids. But why was he even married to that bitter bitch? Either way, it stabs me in the gut thinking about how it all went down for those poor bastards. All I'm trying to do is have a good time before judgement day. So, I patronize the pussy and demonize the dick, and then the loose and easy get down, dirty and sleazy.

But you know what? After all this drunkenness and debauchery, I still haven't had a good time. Ever since I got hooked on whiskey, coke and fucked-up women; every day feels like judgement day. Sadly, my wife is only with me because of her devout faith in the God I only preach about. My kids look up to a fraud. Damn-it, Doc, I'm almost no better than Vanity.

Alright Doc, I'm going to make this real quick and easy for you. I've never seen anybody come to church so religiously yet didn't believe in God. Vanity's death was a mercy killing, she had it coming. That poor family is better off without her and her hell-bound ways. I'll bet she believes in God now, though."

He concluded with one last swig. The preacher then smoothly got up out of the couch, while offering me a drink from his almost empty flask. I politely declined. He gave me a wink and a grin as he opened the office door to exit the scene. "Yeah, you do good business, Doc. Thank you for letting me get that off my chest, and God bless," he said. And though he left the door wide-open, I never saw the preacher again.

"I can't believe you are getting the lobster," BellaRae protests in a weary tone. I suddenly stop the good-looking server before he gets too far away from our table with our picky orders, and I insist, "On second thought, I'll take the crab, instead. Thanks."

Chapter Nine
Clark

"I have seen the burden God has laid on men. He has made every-thing beautiful in its time" (Ecclesiastes 3: 10, 11).

"It's really good to see you again, Clark. I just wish I had better news for you. Please, sit with me for a bit," I started our last session with. Clark had been deeply humbled; to be more precise, utterly broken from his children being kept from him. Politics kept any sort of reunion (even visits) hostage from them, regardless of testimonies in Clark's favor for such a thing. And yet again, I couldn't manage to get even a brief visit for him and his children this Christmas.

"It is great to see you, as well, Doc. Especially, so close to Christmas. Thank you for taking time for this special session. You have been so helpful to me and my children through all of this," he replied after taking his seat. The torment and the pain seething from out of him filled the room and choked me up. It was almost unbearable. It was difficult to remain professional, but I was able to keep from breaking down and sobbing 'I'm so sorry' over and over, again. This time.

Yet he didn't let on. He didn't seem to fall into the murky pit of all the grim shit surrounding him. Instead, he presented a grateful affect; almost as though he found a way to triumph over all his ferocious heartache—like he knew something we didn't. It appeared to me with all the heavy burden and broken spirit Clark was lugging around; he was somehow giving me a Christmas gift in this session. His graceful attitude deranged my perspective on everything and made me rethink my own values and priorities.

"My sister Sandy gave me excellent news a couple of days ago. Speaking of Christmas gifts. She told me Pastor Grope's church donated enough funds to allot her and her family (husband, Richard, along with their two girls, Cassandra and Denise) enough money to purchase a house large enough for Grace and David to stay too. Apparently, they are to be released over to her custody next year. The good thing about it is they will get to be with family this season, because of the courts allowing Grace and David a visitation with my sister and her family on Christmas Day. Sandy has visited Grace and David every day, ever since they were seized by the state.

And stranger yet, Pastor Grope himself has insisted on covering the rest of the expenses like food, clothes, and education for my kids. It takes me out at the knees, every time I think about everything they have been through. Everything is so meaningless without them; I miss them so damned much. Please thank Pastor Grope for me?" Clark sincerely requested.

"Yeah, you bet, Clark," I responded. I added, "Is there anything through all of this you would like to impart to the judge, in order to provoke some sort of leniency from her? Is there a message I might give your kids, perhaps to ease some of the soreness of this holiday?"

"Thank you, Bill. There certainly is," he eagerly replied. "Please, tell Grace and David I am most remorseful for not being there for them when they needed me most. If you don't take the time to recognize your regrets, your regrets will take the time to recognize you. Also, tell them I know full well in every situation, every circumstance, and every interaction, I could have been a bit kinder. More attentive. And most of all, tell them how much they mean to me—tell them how much I love them."

I asked, "And any words for the judge? Any thoughts, and/or feelings regarding Vanity?" Clark answered my legal inquiry with concise clarity, "Bill, to slay the dragon and lay the monster to rest was one of the kindest things I could have done for my children. In fact, it was the best thing Vanity ever did for them. For what it's worth, Doc, you are just as crazy as I am; and you know it. The most solid proof I have is you are walking this planet by choice every mad day. Every mad season. Like imbeciles we rip, tear and claw for peace-of-mind on a planet chalked-full of lunatics. Only the sane die young, my friend." After his arresting words, Clark crossed his arms then closed his eyes to an inner chuckle which delicately cocked his head back and produced a small, but sincere smile. He (and I, along with my unprofessional snicker) for one moment—a holy moment—had an instant vacation. But only for a moment. We were both refreshed with a mercifully twisted sigh-of-relief.

When he opened his sleepless eyes, there I witnessed a glimmer of delight, and a slight tear. Only for a moment. The guard knocked on the door to let us know Clark's time was almost up. So we concluded the session. "Thank you, Doc, and Merry Christmas," he summed up. I wasn't supposed to, but I gave Clark a hug. It felt like I would never see him again. Then, according to protocol,

I called the guard in. The guard gently shackled Clark for transport back to the bitter climate of the penitentiary to await his last judgement. The guard sympathetically patted Clark on the back and affectionately said, "Okay, Big-Guy, we've got to get going... You drive." Jokingly, the guard concluded, to keep things light for a prisoner he obviously liked. They both gave a friendly nod and a decent smile to each other, like old friends.

Consequently, a couple of days later, Christmas Day, to be exact, I received the phone call informing me the night before (Christmas Eve), Clark had a fatal heart attack. However, he kept a journal on his bunk (I suggested in our early sessions it would be a significant benefit if he utilize such a thing) for therapy, and I keep it for myself until this very day. It comprises mostly blank pages, apart from two words Clark wrote in big-black letters and no punctuation. Directly in the middle of the blank pages it reads: THOROUGHLY EMBARRASSED—

CHAPTER TEN
Comfort for the Afflicted

"Someone painted April Fool in big-black-letters on a Dead End sign, I had my foot on the gas as I left the road and blew out my mind; eight miles out of Memphis and I've got no spare, eight miles straight-up down-town somewhere. I just dropped in to see what condition my condition was in" (Kenny Rogers and The Fifth Edition).

"For what it's worth, Bill, the crab was an excellent choice. While we were all planning this year's shindig, we took a vote which brought us to the conclusion we must have steak and lobster to feast on, regardless of your traditional defiance," BellaRae gracefully offers. I perk up with a better attitude and confirm, "Hey, that all sounds terrific. What a smart decision. It's best we don't get stuck on well-worn paths, right? So, thank you." After eating, we quickly pay our bill, leaving a fat tip for our pretty-boy server. It assists in keeping us safer in any given society when we reward our service workers. We have always been prudent enough to pay our servers well. It seems to make life abundantly less menacing to sow the right seeds. Because in the end, make no mistake, we all reap what we sow.

Sluggishly full, we stroll out to our cars, accompanied by light-hearted jokes and jabs. We all remark on our warm feelings and fond memories sparked by the freshly fallen snow. The kids inform BellaRae and I they are going straight back to the house to get some rest. Just as I am about to share my altruistic news of needing to still get Casey Morris a sympathy gift (a weak attempt to impress my loved ones) unexpectedly, BellaRae asserts, "I just purchased tickets for Casey and his family to go to the truck races, at the Speedway this June. I remember overhearing him and his brother saying how much they would love to go watch the big trucks race, someday. I recall their dad also saying it would be fun. One more confirmation on my phone, and BOOLUA! Now, let's go home and hang-out with our kids."

"We should probably go to the novelty store and get him a card, as well. Don't you think it would be more personalized?" I pretentiously whine back. BellaRae's recourse is a good-hearted acquiesce, "That is exactly what that poor-boy needs, is some good-natured sympathy. Alright, Bill, let's do this. I'll drive." We get to the store in five minutes, tops. Within the flurry of cute Christmas cards, we fortunately locate one themed GET WELL SOON. We pay for the good deed and leave the store with no fuss; kind card in hand and truck tickets en route—all within five minutes, tops.

At this point, we decide we might as well stop over at the Morris home and drop the caring card off, along with the exciting news regarding the truck tickets. "Besides," we say to each other, "It isn't that late, and it is the weekend—Christmas weekend." BellaRae and I realize we can also take this opportunity to wish them all a 'Merry Christmas,' as good neighbors ought. When all is said and done, with a clear conscience we can go home and lock all these filthy bastards out while we take shelter with the ones we love and trust the most.

BellaRae and I arrive at the Morris' home (which is only across the street from ours) in a quick minute. As we anxiously take turns signing the card, I can see the Morris boys scurrying to the heavily decorated front door to see who it might be. Shamelessly staring at us as we approach, the Morris kids survey us out through the front door window. BellaRae and I stroll up the charmingly lit walkway towards their door. She rings the doorbell, while I stand behind her with a fraudulently stupid smile on my face. Casey answers the door and estimating by the sincere look of glee smothered all over his pimple-infested face, he had been longing for some outside company. And since it's only BellaRae and I, he's obviously grateful for just about anybody to stop by.

"Hey, guys," Casey greets. "Don't you two live across the street?" Indeed, his inquiry goes to show how neighborly neighbors are these days. "Yeah, you knuckle-head; it's us nerds from across the street. How's your broken wing?" BellaRae jest-fully returns with a sporty smile. "The word on the street is that you broke your arm taking on the legendary snow-jump. So, we thought we should stop by to wish you well with this card and truck-racing tickets to follow; your thoughts?" BellaRae, cheerfully plays. I can honestly testify from personal experience; she has always been a friend to the foolish.

Casey's little brother was right beside him when we delivered the exciting news. Meanwhile, Casey's younger brother frantically starts jumping around and joyfully yelling gibberish; Casey's jaw drops as he shouts, "Please! Come in! Mom! Dad! The Hyneez-itzs are here from across the street! They got us a cool Christmas present! Hurry!" Cocktails in hand, the Morris parents (Lynn and

Keith) casually strut slowly towards the entrance to politely, and with politically correct accuracy, greet us. I can easily discern they are not genuinely glad to see us, just demonstrating how socially chic they are.

In keeping with smiling faces and a slight slur to their welcoming speech, Lynn, and Keith pitch a (convincingly) friendly presentation. I jot down a few mental notes for myself, so I might improve upon some of my own social displays. "Happy Holidays, Mr. and Mrs. Hyneezitzs; would you like to come in for a drink?" Lynn politely asks, as Keith holds his position with an unrepentant smile, upstaging his merciless glossed-over stare. Creepy. Note to self; not a social vantage-point.

Before we can decline in a friendly manner, Casey excitedly spouts-out, "Mom! Dad! They bought us truck-racing tickets, cause' I got my arm busted going over that big jump!" The Morris parents sip their cocktails, while their blank stares become even more uncomfortable; and with their toothy smiles Lynn reacts, "Well, bless your hearts. What a friendly gesture. Yeah, boys will be boys, right? Thank you so very much. Sorry you can't stay for a bit; we'll have to get together, soon."

BellaRae returns (with a tone of relief), "You bet. Thank you for letting us drop this by to you so late in the evening. Merry Christmas to you, good folks. Have a splendid night." We gently turn towards our home, holding each other's hands, and we gratefully walk back to our humble abode. Our sanctuary. Our shelter from the storms. It only takes us a pleasant moment.

Through thick and thin BellaRae has remained a source of strength and assurance for our children, and me. She has enriched my life in so many ways, but she has more than helped keep me clean and sober for thirty-six years. Clark passing away without him or his children seeing each other one last time was the last straw for me in those foul days. So, I lost hope in his children's well-being. In addition, I lost trust and confidence in our modern humanity. I lost sight of proper perspective and gave up on my ability to help others. Ultimately, I lost all sense of purpose and meaning. But at the time I had enough money tucked away, enough to get by on for at least a couple of years. So, I quit Creedmoor; my career made little sense in my disturbed mind.

I hit the bottle just as much (and as hard) as I popped-prescription-pills (prescribed- the great justification). Without question, I became a full-blown alcoholic/addict. My biggest addictions were self-pity and resentment. The never-ending hole which is never satisfied and never full. And nothing tastes better with alcohol and narcotics than bitterness. In the end, all I wanted, and all I craved was more. Just a bit more.

I was a coward. I hid in the illusions of hiding from life's realities, tucked away in my pompous New York apartment; an apartment my parents ultimately paid for. I lived irresponsibly for approximately three years. Far too long I didn't answer my phone, and I refused to answer my door. My mindless stubbornness bound me from replying to any cards or letters of concern. However, I was narcissistic enough to listen to the messages on the machine; watch through the peephole as a concerned soul would knock on my door; and of course, I kept and obsessively read all the caring cards and letters. I did everything at night, while during the day I would morbidly gaze at Clark's journal and drink myself into a calloused, poor me. It felt heroic to suffer alone. I was sick.

I was depraved and desperately lonely. Until an old colleague of mine from Creedmoor whom I genuinely loved and respected, left an irresistibly compelling piece of information on my freshly erased message-machine. "Hey Bill. This is Dick—Dick Wild. Your old friend from college, BellaRae, has been in contact with me for a little over a month. I've told her about the condition you've been in ever since you left your position here at Creedmoor. She's been attempting to track you down, so she located me and asked if I could reach-out to you and see if I could help get you two connected. She wants to see you, Bill. We want to help. Please, contact me at my office number or at my home phone, anytime. My home number is area code..." BEEEEEEEEEEEP!

Some sort of spark spooked my shadows as I continuously over-played his message. It was like two slippery stones were ferociously beaten against each other, creating a bright and beautiful flame in a deeply dark and humid place. Hell, I hadn't seen or heard from BellaRae since our date in 1976. I'd missed her. I thought about her every single day; without fail, I would fantasize about us getting married someday. As far as I was concerned, I was in love with her. But why no contact until now? I didn't care; I wanted to see her. I had to see her.

How soothing it was to my tormented soul to hear Dr. Wild's voice. The very next day, after I polished off the rest of the Jack Daniels I didn't finish the night before, along with a couple more pills, I called Dr. Wild at his longstanding office number. He answered on the first ring, "Dick here. What can I do to help you?"

I explained to Dr. Wild how I was more than interested in getting in contact with BellaRae. Just hearing her name, and Dr. Wild reaching out to me was already lighting a way out of the dark alley I was stuck in all those doomed and foul-smelling years. He gave me her office and home phone numbers. In addition, he gave me an address and directions to her office. My fried mind was concocting a grandiose reunion, one in which my limited thinking saw it best to surprise her with a cliché Romantic Comedy entrance; and then we ride off into the sunset. Instead of calling her home phone, I called her office phone where I could speak to her receptionist and book an appointment.

I made an appointment with the nice receptionist under the false name, Clyde Wilhelm. I thought everything was poised for an epic reacquaintance. However, I neglectfully overlooked one minor detail, BellaRae was now a polished professional.

And then the day came when I was due to attend the expected appointment with the woman I've obsessed upon, since the first day I'd seen her. Meanwhile, I had already started cutting back on my drug problems and my heavy drinking, mostly. I was so eager to see her I couldn't keep my damaged head on straight. Multiple times, I considered abandoning the appointment. I had no more confidence and absolutely no certainty. My own delusional fears deranged me, but somehow, I followed through with the appointment.

Her office was on the third floor of a charming old building in downtown New York; midtown Manhattan, dead center on 50th street. When I reached the third floor, I knew I was in the right place because of the sign on the door with big-black letters, reading: COMFORT FOR THE AFFLICTED. Along with a phone number to call anytime anybody needed help. My heart was racing out of my bony chest as I opened the door to the reception area. I entered to see an incredibly old woman sitting to the left of me on the waiting room couch, reading the day's newspaper.

I'd say she was at least in her early eighties, very well-dressed with copious amounts of make-up about her face, ears and neck. Judging by the stuffed ashtray of lipstick covered cigarette-butts, she was a chain-smoker; in fact, she was smoking while I made this assessment. Not once did she look up. While on the right-side of my peripheral vision (the 'nice' receptionist I spoke with on the phone) was a noticeably confident, somewhat snarky, full-figured black woman. She too wore lots of make-up and wore very revealing attire. She was mesmerizing.

If the beautiful black woman had a name tag, I would have attempted to charm for some of her favor; however, I could tell she didn't like white folks too much. For instance, every time she answered the phone with her sweet and accommodating tone and the caller had a miserably stereotypical white name, she would organically roll her eyes and nod her head in quiet disapproval. Yet, she always sounded professional. And nice.

At any rate, I twinkle-toed my way over to her sharply organized desk. I cautiously approached with a friendly smile on my over-privileged, pale face. I stood at the front of her desk, while she rapidly scanned me up and down. Behind her professional smile were all the neon signs of utter disappointment. Immediately following an uncontrollable eye-roll, she raised her condescending eyebrows and inquired, "Are you supposed to be Clyde, Clyde Whatever?" She then lit a cigarillo right as I answered, "Yes, Mam. Clyde Wilhelm, to be exact."

"Sit your jive-ass down, Bill. We know you're the shifty asshole who booked an appointment under false pretenses. The good Dr. will be ready for you in a brief moment. Lying to me with a stone-cold, straight face pasted on your ugly mug. You're doped-out and you've been drinking, I have a good mind to smack you up alongside your drunk-ass numb-skull!" She snapped back. The kindly old lady sitting on the couch (whom I was about to sit next to) was joyfully chuckling to herself.

Frightened, I recklessly pulled the dirty white-privilege card and demanded the curvy black woman give me her name, 'at once' (as if I had some sort of clout). With which she, cool and calm as a summer breeze, picked up a fresh notepad, and a finely sharpened pencil, then strongly suggested, "You're going to want to write this down, sukkah. And I'm only going to tell you one time; now make certain you let this rattle around in your empty head. Don't forget...None of your got-damned business! Now, sit your candy-ass down, shut your troublemaking hole and wait your damned turn!" The old lady I had to sit next to lit another cigarette and continued to chuckle.

Meanwhile, the strong receptionist's glare never left my position the rest of the time I uncomfortably spent in the waiting area. Even when she would answer the phone or jot down a message, her stony stare kept me caged. It took at least twenty minutes before BellaRae rung for me. "The doctor will see you now, 'Clyde What-ever'," the woman in charge said, while the eloquently dressed old lady resumed her hard-earned chortle. I was surrounded; they outnumbered me.

Nervously, I timidly but rapidly tapped on BellaRae's office door. "She's expecting you, dumb-ass. Move forward already," the old lady decisively chimed in with an all-too-familiar eye roll. No more false-humility, no more false-pride, no more resistance. I had to go in.

"B.J.! It's me, Pops!" I bellowed like a rabid ape with a toothy smile on my savage face. And we met the explosively grandiose reunion I had imagined up to this juncture with something more appropriate. Something genuine. With a sobering look on her cultivated face, BellaRae looked up from her notes she'd been briefing at her large eighteen-hundreds desk. She gently got up from her desk, gracefully walked over to me and with tears welling up in her weathered eyes she embraced me. We partook in a painful sigh of relief. Only for a moment.

But then the painfully pleasant warm-fuzzies abruptly discontinued. BellaRae wiped away the tearstains from about her eyes, cheeks, and lips; she looked me dead in my pathetic eyes and stated, "Okay Bill, please, sit down so we can get started." I slithered into the well-cushioned leather-bound seat (positioned in front of her desk) with the poise of a strung-out carnie. Shifty-eyed and twitchy.

She went on to say, "Dr. Wild cared enough about your well-being that he kindly typed up a generous amount of context regarding your defiant self-pity, which lead to your self-destructive spiral descent." "Self-pity?!" I protested. "Yeah, self-pity," She responded.

"The self-indulgent arrogance of taking on bigger cases than anybody should tackle on their own, like a damned fool. Sick people are not here for your ego inflation. And when you're unable to prove to everyone what an amazing superhero, you are in your world; you sulk in the delusions of nobody understanding how 'smart' and 'special' you are. Thus, you drink and drug yourself into a maliciously moronic martyrdom. In fact, you are only here out of desperate loneliness, while you have no fucking clue on how to make a connection. As much as I understand your condition, the charade is over, Bill.

It is in your best interest to get into a recovery program. You will connect to other recovering addicts, alcoholics, and co-dependents. Also, you will go to counseling, just like the rest of us, and you will get a sponsor. Then after a year of deep cleaning, some deep mending, and some sobriety; we will move our relationship forward. In fact, I've been clean and sober for ten years now."

She reached into the top-drawer of her desk and pulled out what looked like a small sign with a hangman's noose tied to it, "Starting today, you will wear this beautiful necklace around your neck for the next ninety days." The sign glowed in big florescent-green letters: NO EXCUSES.

"Today, you will attend your first meeting with your mouth shut. You will escort the nicely dressed, chain-smoking angel out there in the waiting room, to said meeting. She is my sponsor and will make you feel secure with what is next. Without her help, I wouldn't be clean and sober. She inspires me to inspire others. You see, Bill, I'm a recovering sex-addict with a severe case of control issues. When I first discovered recovery, my sponsor always said, 'The fear of the Lord is the beginning of wisdom'. That being said, if God doesn't terrify you by now, not even a proctologist who specializes in rotting-head removals can help you, now."

And so it is. I indulged in the rotting-head extraction; it's excruciating. Getting well takes time. I have been clean and sober for thirty-six years. With a great deal of help from those who have my best interest in mind and heart, I certainly did get better. We got married, and on my birthday, so I would not forget. Only the vexing echoes sucker-punch me every now and again. Nevertheless, I am painfully grateful. I truly have a good life; especially on paper. Yet, like a broken toe, I just didn't heal quite right.

CHAPTER ELEVEN
Over the Hill

"That it will never come again, is what makes Life so sweet" (Emily Dickinson).

Early recovery for me was like teaching a brick how to swim, or float on its back. I was passively resistant every step in the right direction. One stirring and dear thing I keep locked tight in my 'Lest-Ye-Forget' savings-account, however, is something incredibly special my philosophy instructor stated way back in my college days; he challenged, "When habits change, reality changes." Regardless of whether or not we enjoy it, those tempering words remain indisputably accurate.

This year's celebration is a precious time we take to smother each other with gratitude. And gratitude never arrives empty-handed. We appreciate how imperative thankfulness is to the health and wellbeing of one's heart, mind, soul, and spirit. Perhaps even the neighbors and the community. Maybe not. Either way, we have a good time.

As it stands, here we are huddled up together, peacefully enjoying a mindless holiday comedy on the boob-tube, just before bed. Just right. It's midnight, and BellaRae gets up to kiss everybody on the forehead, accompanied with a conscious effort to tell each one of us how special we are and how much she loves us. She gets to me, and from her toasty bath-robe pocket cleverly presents a four-inch by eight-inch lockbox (in the shape of a treasure-chest) with a green skull painted on the side of it. Playfully she asks, "Remember this?" as she hands the mysterious container to me. Kissing me goodnight, she leaves the key to the small lockbox in my mouth. Then BellaRae struts-off to bed.

I tuck the curious box into my robe before the kids take notice and push to examine the contents with me. Nope, this is mine. I quietly mumble 'goodnight' to the crew and commence scampering-off to the main bathroom. On entering the restroom, I gingerly lock the door behind me. I kept the lockbox key between my cheek and gum where BellaRae left it. For no damned good reason, I tiptoe over to the vanity counter and place the box in front of the lit-up mirror, unlock the mysterious contraption and expose the contents. There it is. My eyes light up like a Christmas tree as I gaze in wonder at what BellaRae just gave me for our thirty-seventh anniversary.

I haven't seen this little game changer since 1976; Sandoz Laboratories, LD-25—LSD. And in the original vile. The same container of pure liquid lysergic-acid diethylamide BellaRae used to 'break-the-ice' on our first date. And she kept it all this time; how romantic. But why now? What is her design? Design?

Funny, it feels like it's already working...Gripes! The lid is loose; it is, in fact, working. Not good, it is past midnight, and we have a big day tomorrow with guests and everything. We must get up early for preparations! I can't mess up our day with such gross negligence! Okay, calm down, Hyneezitzs. First, I'll shut this lid, tightly. Second, I need to wipe the rest of the liquid from the outside of this vile. And lastly, I need to focus.

Perhaps I can get to bed and fall asleep before this stuff takes a firm hold. I just hope I can traverse the travail of finding my way out of this bathroom without making things pointlessly dramatic. But I also need to beeline it through the hallway (which is riddled with sentimental family photos), climb all the way up the stairs, take a quick right towards our bedroom and then some much needed rest. All I need now is the follow-through. This stuff has already championed my senses. I can't even get my clammy hand on the door handle before completely forgetting what I want to do next; mostly because these constant oddities I see keep overtaking my knowledge of time and space. Focus, dammit.

Before I exit this lavatory, I must properly wash my hands and wipe this residue from my pasty face. Note to self: Remember to not look in the mirror. My body feels floaty, funky, and somewhat difficult to navigate. Don't overthink it, Bill. Eek-ads! There it is, my hideous reflection—fright night.

Maybe a bit of BellaRae's make-up might aid me in covering this homely mug, there-by keeping myself free from the embarrassing exposure of being too high. A little here and a little there; it almost seems like I can't get enough on. Knock! Knock! Knock! "Dad? Are you still in there? Dad?" Samantha investigates at the door. "Yeah, Sweetie...Huh, I'm just having a quick soak before bed. Is everything alright out there?" I anxiously reply.

"Yeah, everybody else went to bed an hour ago, and I was waiting for you to get out of the bathroom so I could say 'goodnight'. Also, I wanted to be the first one to wish you a 'happy birthday'. Happy birthday, Dad...You sound funny; are you alright? It's almost three in the morning, you know?" She surveys with concern.

"Shit, yeah! I'm rad! I must have lost track of time!" Loudly and rapidly I return. "Thank you, honey…I'll be heading to bed pretty soon. You should go get some rest too; we have a big day in a couple of hours. I love you, dear." We affectionately and officially finish yelling 'goodnight' to each other through the locked door, when I realize I've barricaded myself in the main bathroom for at least two hours. Unfortunately, I am nowhere near a proper state to make this tricky trek down the hall and up the stairs. But how I am so ready to hide in BellaRae's welcoming arms.

Safety and security; sanctuary. As it stands, I have plenty of make-up on, it's four o'clock in the morning and the bathroom is a disaster closing in on me. I best be going right this instant. Okay, down the hall and up these stairs and here we are. I'd better take care not to wake BellaRae with my nonsense.

"What is that atrocious smell? Oh, hey; what's up, Twisted Sister? You look like you were beaten and taken advantage of with an over-sized ugly stick. Multiple times! Let me guess, you accidently got it into your system somehow, and you've been frying balls all night. Besides this, Bill, it is a quarter after five in the fucking morning and we need to be bright-eyed and bushy-tailed in approximately four hours. In case you've forgotten, we have anticipated celebrations to attend today." My wife gracefully challenges.

My mind attempted to run and hide in several differing directions, only to land in multiple dimensions. As astounding as this experience has become, I find I can only reply to my tolerant wife with, "Yep." She strongly suggests, "Since you already have your clothes off, please, go into our bathroom and soak in a warm bath for a while. Also, while you are in there, put a lot of soap on a washcloth and see if you can scrub some of that freaky ass make over, off. Go. Now."

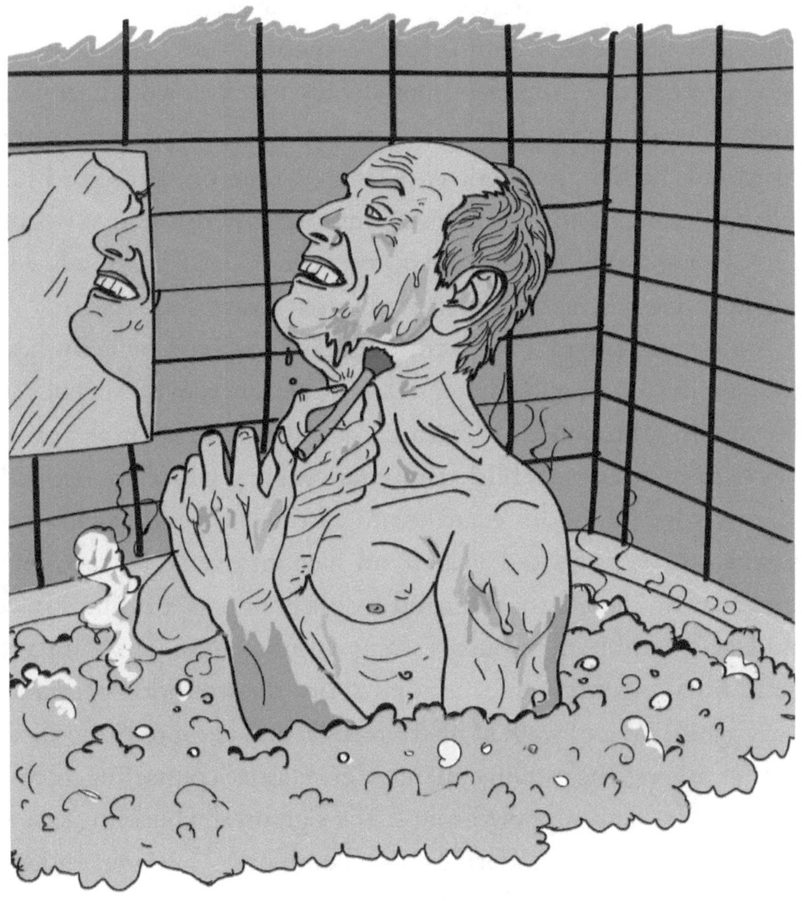

I promptly employ her instructions. While repeating, "Focus, focus, focus," to myself, I somehow get into a warm tub per strong recommendation. Splendid idea, indeed. Animation and relaxation, along with fluttering strands of rabbit-hole contemplations; but getting lost in these rabbit-holes can be a bit of a strain on one's concentration. "Are you contemplating getting your pruned-over body out of that damned tub sometime soon? You've given me your word five different times already that you would get your slimy ass ready for our holiday soiree. It is now one pm, Grace and David will be here in about two hours. Come on! Let's go, Bill!" BellaRae explains to me. It seems my meticulous mantra (focus, focus, focus) is not helping me stay on task. BellaRae certainly will help keep me on track; I am excited to see Grace and David.

Grace and David. I am astonished and inspired by how these two have overcome and conquered some treacherously cruel obstacles in life. Through their hard-earned PHDs in mental health, they have built and establish a foundation for the broken to mend. Pastor Grope left all his extra 'earnings' to Grace and David—the 'earnings' he kept tucked away in an account overseas—before he passed away. He left them a solid five million. As a result, Grace and David combined resources along with BellaRae, Dr. Wild and me to build a functioning, secure facility for wounded people of every age group and walk of life to recover and learn to bring those tools to others. The establishment offers classes, counseling, recovery programs, and support groups. The sign on the building says it all: Healing Grace Foundation. It's a community favorite. In fact, for the community we host functions such as dances, carnivals, farmer's markets, and meals for all the major holidays. No charge.

"Bill!" My wife pleads. "You need to get ready, right now. Please, focus. We have a great deal to be thankful for and celebrate. Most of those obvious reasons are hanging out downstairs wondering what's taking you so long. I can cover stupidity for only a couple of more minutes. The time has come, Pops! Drape yourself, man. And for the love of all that is ugly, wipe the overworked hooker paint off your befuddled face. Thank you, Bill. Be down in ten minutes!" Suddenly, my body heads in the right direction. Abruptly, my faculties engage BellaRae's clear and concise instructions.

Ding-dong! Grace and David have arrived. I have no time to get this makeup off properly. But I need to get my soggy body in some dry attire at once! Unfortunately, nothing is slipping on me quickly or easily except for this blue muumuu, which should blend in charmingly. I am out of time. Okay, deep breath and down we go. Focus, Bill, focus.

I am optimistically certain there will be little to no attention directly on me; due to all the social stimuli unravelling with tonight's festivities. I'll simply duck into the dining area—which smells stunning—and just blend in as though I've been mingling this whole time. Right? Wrong. Upon the last stretch of my anxious journey, the last corner before I enter the dining room, I overhear BellaRae topping off an explanation regarding my predicament, "Alright folks, please listen up, Pops is on his way down; now try not to stare or laugh, because he gets overly sensitive when he's on acid." Chuckles fill the air.

I turn the corner to find the dining area is completely full, and everybody's wide eyes organically scan me up and down. Jaws drop, laced with morbid intrigue, and smothered in entertaining disgust. "Merry Christmas, everybody! When did you get here?" I spastically shout as my false teeth jet out of my mouth (with very red lipstick all over them) and clamber across the table, only to be subdued in a melted bowl of butter for the lobster tails.

BellaRae greets with a snarky undertow, "Well, Bill, you're just in time for the steak and lobster soiree, so it's a good thing you brought your teeth." Meanwhile, all fingers point at me along with an entourage of gut-busting laughter. Congruity! David, through his teared over a red face of glee, wittingly asserts, "What a lovely dining gown! It really accents the brick-red lipstick and dark-blue eyeshadow running down through your sweaty foundation!"

Naturally, the standard paranoia which occurs while encountering much of anything amid a high-powered acid trip, immediately escalates with the hostile takeover of embarrassment. Without batting a caked over eyelash, I run and hide in the garage where I might collect my thoughts and gain some composure. But I spot the old red toboggan we have kept decoratively hung in our garage for all these years. The nostalgic charm tickles my sentimental nerve with a grand idea.

Redeem my pride with something extraordinary, and a thrilling story to tell my family. I am convinced that this is my destiny. Just load this old thing into our vehicle... Sears Hill, I'm coming for you. I'll drive extra carefully, and with the stereo loud enough to drown out the echoes of their hysterical laughter. For a slight moment, I realize that this is silly; crazy, really.

Whatever...I am here now, and how fortunate, it doesn't appear as though any witnesses are around; I can finally do something embarrassment free today. Apart from some dipshit at the bottom of the hill. I yell down at the stupid shadow (while frantically waving my hands high in the thin air), "The line starts up here, moron! Merry Christmas! You, miserable son-of-a-bitch! Ho! Ho! Ho!" Okay, I'm obviously a tad angry. After taking my unchecked resentments out on an undeserving soul, I straddle the ole sled and then fall wrinkled ass down on it. Which pelts me down the slippery slope, and I didn't even get another chance to beg God one last time to give me some sort of convincing sign not to do this.

Ironically, the mysterious shadow at the bottom of the hill starts frantically waving back at me, but with something in his hand. The winter breeze rapidly evolves into a face blistering, frozen gust. My makeup scrambles to the back of my head. And I can attest with great conviction while I mindlessly fall down this fatally icy suicide slick, I have no blazing flames of glory shooting from my amplified eyes. No feelings of adventure, nor no top-of-the-world fulfillment. No stories of achievement and no satisfaction. Nope! Just a sense of gross regret. Right now, there is no doubt in my mind I ought to enjoy some quality time with my loved ones.

Without question, I am a fool. This is completely ridiculous; this is meaningless. I am too old and tired for my own trivial bullshit. Schwhoop! Airborne! My body trembles in fear and burns with trepidation shooting through the razor-sharp air. But flying over the mystery figure, I can finally identify who it is. It's Solomon! Solomon? And he's waving today's paper at me—today's news. I squint my eyes and strain to see through my freezing tears to read the headline, "Wake Up, Little Suzy, Wake Up!" 'Little Suzy?', I wonder to myself. What? Solomon yells at me with delightful urgency, "You are about to hit bottom, sukkah!" Then finally, POP!

CHAPTER TWELVE
Then It Gets Strange

"I'm stunned every day when I go outside, and it isn't a riot with everything burning…It's a miracle that all this stuff works. That all of you crazy chimpanzees—who don't know each other—can sit in the same room for two hours, sweltering away, without tearing each other apart. Because that's what chimps do" (Jordan B. Peterson).

Husband: "Wake up, Suzy. Suzy! Suzy, wake up!"

Young kids: "Mama, mama, get up. Mama, we're hungry!"

Eldest daughter (teenager): "Come on already, Sue. Let's go! My friends and I are meeting up, later (you, selfish bitch). Geeze!"

Husband: "Honey, wake up; Dr. Johnson called. She left a message stating they've come to a resolve regarding your meeting last week before we left. Come on Suzy, it's time to wake up."

Suzy: "Alright, already, I'm up; I'm up. What?"

Eldest daughter: "Geeze, you don't have to be such a jag, Sue."

Dad: "Grace, show some respectful decency toward your mother. She has been under a tremendous amount of stress the last couple of years from being deeply tied up in her work. Meanwhile, she has provided a comfortable life for us; you should be thankful."

Grace: "Sorry, Sue."

Young kids (twins): "Mama, we wanted to eat something, but daddy made us wait for you!"

Suzy: "Alright, guys. Please, give me just a few minutes to gather myself so I may address each of you properly. Good morning and I love you. Okay? Except for you, babe; I think I have some debriefing to do. If you get a chance, would you forfeit a few minutes of your busy schedule and give me some ear-time?"

Husband: "Absolutely, just let me help Grace get Jourdan and Tammy settled down with some breakfast, and I'll be right back in to hear you out."

Grace: "What?"

Dad: "That's right, we have to get into the giving spirit, Christmas is next week. Okay, you guys, let's get you something to eat. Come on, Grace. Would you like me to bring you anything when I return?"

Suzy: "Sure. I'll take an extraordinarily strong piping-hot cup of joe. Thank you, sweetie."

Dad: "Grace, get your mom a fresh mug of coffee. Please and thank you."

Grace: "Fug, alright. Fine!"

Dad: "Thanks again, champ."

Suzy: "Well done, Grace. Is your dad on his way in, yet?"

Grace: "Yeah, queenie; and you're welcome."

Husband: "Alright beautiful, the kids are eating in front of the tube and I see that Grace already brought your coffee in. Now, before we discuss the expected phone call, please, share with me what's been bogging you down this morning. But first, here, take your meds."

Suzy: "BellaRae called with the final resolve to the matter?"

Bill: "It certainly seemed that way, but due to legal constraints, she couldn't disclose any significant details to me."

Suzy: "Actually, my disturbing dream was brought about by something confidential; the dreadful Hyneezitzs case. Damn! Just the name alone overwhelms me with anxiety; it's just so complicated and a heinous burden to bear."

Bill: "Stop it, we are on a fun family vacation, just take your medications."

Suzy: "Good idea. But anyway, I dreamt I was Hyneezitzs. Not in the realm of how he lives day-to-day, but the life his broken and delusional mind has convinced him he has fully experienced; and is experiencing. You see, Bill, Solomon Hyneezitzs has been institutionalized since he was five. He's now 36 years of age; yet, without question, he believes he is sixty-five and retired. As you know, this case has consumed me for years and taken me away from what's important. Which is why the results of this meeting are so valuable to our future; for what's next."

Bill: "BellaRae stressed how we must enjoy our well-earned family holiday, vacation. Also, she needs you to return her phone call at your nearest convenience. The answer to what is next is only a phone call away."

Suzy. "Alright."

Grace: "Mom, are you going to get out of bed anytime soon? I want to get back home already."

Dad: "Yeah, sweetie. Mom and I are mostly packed. We will get going after your mother attends to this short, but particularly important phone call."

Suzy: "I best get to it. Unfortunately, we probably should get home. I'd rather spend Christmas here, though. It's been a great get-away. Grace, will you please help Tammy and Jourdan get cleaned up, packed and ready to go? Thank you."

Grace: "Whatever."

Dad: "I'll be in to help in just a few minutes, Gracey. Thank you."

Suzy: "Okay, we have two hours before check out; I just wish we could stay for a couple more weeks. Will you sit with me while I make this call, Bill?"

Bill: "Of course, dear. Remember, you are a professional. Sure, you may have fried a couple twisted wires working on this long and arduous case; but you know damned-well the kids and I love and support you. In like manner, you sure as shit know BellaRae and Dr. Wild love you and have your best interest in mind. They too, have labored over Hyneezitzs and have suffered the mental anguish of his troublesome case. Suzy, you know everything is going to work out for the best."

Suzy: "You're right, Bill. Here it goes."

Grace: "Alright, mom and dad, Jourdan and Tammy are all cleaned up. They are mostly packed-up and are now quietly watching School House Rock videos on YouTube. How did the phone call go? Are we actually leaving?"

Dad: "Thank you, Grace; that was quick and efficient. No, to answer one of your questions, mom has not made the call yet."

Suzy: "Right now, dear. I'll put her on speakerphone."

BellaRae (answers the phone, first ring): "Dr. Johnson, here. How may I help you today?"

Suzy: "BellaRae, it's me, Dr. Sowschitts."

BellaRae: "Susan, I am so glad you returned my phone call, so soon—how are you doing?"

Suzy: "Actually, I'm doing much better. The much-needed family time has been enriching with this wonderful ski-trip; We can't thank you enough. I'm just anxious to learn the final analysis."

BellaRae: "Yes, of course. Right out of the gate, I want you to rest assured that this whole thing concludes with you and your family's best interest at the heart of it. As you well know, Dr. Wild and I have both tackled the Hyneezitzs case within our careers. We too, have been deformed in one way or another from laboring over the menacing and mean spirited Hyneezitzs case. By the Providence beyond ourselves, we have overcome the mental anguish of such a tragic patient; and you will too."

Suzy: "Well, that's good news. I certainly appreciate your agile comprehension on this front."

BellaRae: "Absolutely, now for our final decision regarding your future role at Creedmoor. We have agreed to a medical retirement, an honorable one. The committee concludes this is what's best for you, your family, and our practically untreatable patient, Solomon Hyneezitzs. When you are better, we would like to leave an open-ended opportunity for you to co-create and orchestrate a new program with us. A safe place for counsellors, clergy, psychiatrists, and psychologists alike to vent and purge the darker demons we have experienced within our practices, to mend. Thus, equipping ourselves with a well-rounded and well-armored approach to just about anything we struggle through within our careers, and our lives."

Suzy: "I am humbled by the administration's gratuitous grace upon your final verdict. Thank you, BellaRae."

BellaRae: "Actually, it was Dr. Wild who championed this retirement arrangement for you. I simply brought the proper attitude and insightful tenacity to streamline this thing. Just between you and me, though, I've asked Dr. Wild how he seems to stay so centered and grounded. An undeniable calm and certainty in strange times. He responded with rigorous conviction, "It's level ground at the cross," he said. At any rate, please be cautious with your prescribed medications. We shall see you in a month for your exit meeting and retirement party. We love you, Susan; enjoy the rest of your family vacation and Merry Christmas."

Suzy: "Merry Christmas, BellaRae. I'll see you in a month. Bye. Wow, it feels so relieving to have finally arrived at the end of this matter, in-one-piece too."

Bill: "Grace, Jourdan, Tammy, get unpacked; we're staying through Christmas! Grace, you get to decide where we eat dinner tonight in celebration of your mother's retirement. Just make certain they serve blueberry cheesecake. Right, honey?"

Suzy: "Oh, yeah!"

Bill: "I told you everything would work out for the best."

Suzy: "You sure did."

Grace: "Tammy and Jourdan are playing with their racetrack right now; can we listen to some music while we finish unpacking?"

Dad: "Of course, I'll get it rolling. What would you like to listen to?"

Grace and Suzy: "Black Sabbath!"

Dad: "Ozzy or Dio?"

Grace and Suzy: "Both!"

Grace sings along to one of her favorites, while we continue to unpack for our celebration to a happy ending, "You've nothing to say! And they're breaking away! If you listen to fools: Break the circle and stop the movement, the wheel is thrown to the ground; just remember it might start rolling and take you right back around!"

Compelled by edgy nerves, I block out the song and my daughter's loud singing. For no discernable reason, a grim undertow takes my good mood captive. To avoid any honest internal dialogue, I play the blame game (dammit, Hyneezitzs!). Unfortunately, the resentment exacerbates my depression and triggers only anxiety and sorrow. As I reach into my suitcase for my nice toasty-gloves I get locked into a shadowy memory.

CHAPTER THIRTEEN
Merry Catharsis

*"It is a terrible, an inexorable law that one cannot deny the human-
ity of another without diminishing one's own: in the face of one's
victim, one sees oneself"* (James Baldwin).

"Merry Christmas, Pops, and good morning. Happy birthday, old-timer. Happy anniversary, old friend. Alright,
Bill, it's time to get up," BellaRae gently presents. "I'm uncertain
why you are so tired, because you got into bed and fell fast asleep.
Either way, you were obviously exhausted," she informs me with
light caresses on my head. I repeatedly blink my eyes with relief
and inquire, "Good morning, beautiful; it's Christmas morning?"

"Yeah, silly. You came wondering into bed about an hour after
I got comfortably settled in. You were mumbling some sort of gibberish as you mindlessly circled the room several times, but once
you got under the blankets and snuggled up next to me—you fell
fast asleep. Deep rest, I hope. However, the weird gibberish continued throughout the night; you must have prematurely opened
the anniversary gift. You do realize it was strictly intended for sentimental purposes?" she condescendingly asks with a fun chuckle.

"Why, yes, I did as a matter of fact," I anxiously react. "I opened it. And thankfully, according to your account of last night's festivities, I slept through them all. Which means the vivid nightmare I had was all in my twisted mind. I am so grateful to see your gorgeous face; Merry Christmas and Happy Anniversary!" Oddly, I find myself somewhat saddened by the incomplete feelings I have because of this bad dream.

"I see, birthday boy; you accidently got some into your system. And though you were able to get to bed before the acid hit-hard, the dosage you took brought some of your tucked away unconscious contents and processes to your recognition. Does any of this textbook mumbo jumbo resonate why you are so eager not to share your frightening dream with me?" BellaRae insightfully returns.

"Exactly!" I unwittingly blurt out. "Go on," she offers. "Yeah, sweety, I'm embarrassed to admit I had a strange dream where I was our old friend, Suzy Sowschitts." BellaRae interjects, "My old friend whom I remain in contact with? You used her as just a means-to-an-end?" Which unfortunately is correct.

I lament, "I thought I knew better by now, but I sincerely did not realize how something I'd done so many years ago would affect me in ugly ways, 'til this very day. Reducing her into a caricature, I presumed she would be ill-effected by my false face. I convinced myself her friends were only accessories as far as she was concerned, anyway. Yet, even if it did not affect her in vicious ways, my thoughtless behaviors have affected me in unresolved ways." BellaRae kindly reminds me, "Precisely why it is never prudent to amuse oneself with actions which are against humanity." I continue to purge my ugly dream to her, while she listens attentively with agile comprehension.

Regardless of the chaotic descriptions I disclose to my partner with all the reasonable sanity she gives up in order to analyze me and my dream, BellaRae gets right to the nuts. "What you recklessly considered 'harmless' were acts of narcissistic megalomania," she says, "all of which have damaged you and others. Also, the other is my dear friend you've caused harm towards. And after all this time of denial, it's all caught up to you and now you are getting stung. Bill, for your psychic hygiene, your spiritual gardening, and your well-being, you know damn well you need to make an amends. It's psychotic to minimize someone to an accessory. It's sick to increase suffering."

"You know what?" I resolutely perk up, "you are absolutely correct. In fact, I already feel as though I am carrying a lighter load with the certainty and clarity of resolve. I will reach out to Suzy in order to make an amends. I could send her a message through your Facebook, or I could shoot her a text; do you still have her contact information?"

BellaRae thoughtfully rebuttals, "Of course I have all of Suzy's contact information. We've remained in contact with one another ever since college. She was a good friend to me during those unusual and potentially lonely days of higher education. She even asks how you are doing every time we converse. And, no, you will instead write her a letter. A letter is more personal. More honest. Make no mistake, making an amends for harms done is the only way to forgive ourselves." I agree with tremendous relief.

"Now," she light-heartedly moves on, "Let's go party, it's time to celebrate. Let's go toast our overflowing cups. Ever acknowledging how none of this is about what we can only see with our eyes. It's not about plastic, or store-bought items. It's about appreciating those right in front of you and nurturing faith in a rejuvenated hope which springs forth from an everlasting love." Per usual, she stands firm as the voice of reason.

As a result, just the willingness alone afforded me a very merry Christmas. A fun celebration with the ones I love and deeply value. We all carried on with a great day chalked-full of belly laughs, warm-hearted camaraderie, and newfound fond memories. It remains without dispute; the end of a matter is always better than its beginning. The only thing left is the follow-through, the letter.

CHAPTER FOURTEEN
The Letter

"The less able I am to believe in our epoch and the more arid and depraved mankind seems in my eyes, the less I look to revolution as the remedy and the more I believe in the magic of love" (Hermann Hesse).

December, 25

Dear Suzy,

Happy Hanukkah, Merry Christmas; and an extraordinary New Year to you. I trust this letter has reached you well. Furthermore, I am humbly aware you have not seen or heard from me in quite a long time. I equally recognize what a rude and abrupt departure I made from our close correspondence in college, as though we weren't friends at all. Or, more like, I was not a genuine friend to begin with. Instead, I was self-centered, cowardly, small-minded, disrespectful, and irresponsible to be exact. Dysfunctional. Insufficient funds in the realm of decency.

In fact, if it weren't for the time and attention BellaRae allocates to those she calls friends, this letter, properly due you, would not have made it promptly into your hands. Left to my own devices, I self-destruct: I leave the right things undone, rendering the right words unspoken. We need each other and we need the reassurance we can trust each other for this assurance.

Without the bondage of denial, I would be remiss if I did not diffidently acknowledge the harm I've caused you. Strictly, an account of the misery I have perpetuated through my arrogance, deceit, and resentment. This missive is not a feeble attempt to escape with an unstable 'sorry', but a note of consideration. The presumptuous and over-privileged terminology of 'I'm sorry' is certainly no excuse, nor recompense for such shortcomings. And definitely no way to stand firm for what's right in a demoralizing and demonic world chalked full of people tortured with breaking their own rules.

Quite the contrary, dear soul. It would be overwhelmingly foolish and at my age desperately disappointing to pretend otherwise. Back in the 'good-ole-days' when you sported me a pal by confiding in me as a friend, I failed to reciprocate such splendid relational tack with the same honesty. Pathetically, I was but a clown carrying on as if I could play you for a fool, while diminishing and damaging a better way of life for no damned-good-reason. I've killed time and wounded eternity. And if we truly learn more from our failures than our successes, then I am poised for greatness.

But now I do it differently. Everything. Though I am remorseful for wrongs I've done, I am also grateful BellaRae has remained in contact with you. Like a proper friend. Which puts me at liberty to invite you and your family (as BellaRae has informed me) out for dinner, immediately, this new year. And step forward on building new relations with some familiar and somewhat aged faces. Otherwise, we might miss out on some fun stuff.

In short, it's a mean regret the hideous ways in which I've maltreated you. This letter of reconciliation is only a first step towards an amends to you. For what it's worth, one of my genuine friends (Lou Drew) used to temper my bitching and moaning whenever I would confide in him with my distresses; he would offer me this focal point: "Don't do anything to hurt yourself or anybody else, and everything should be alright." And then he would follow with: "I'm grateful for the pain that got me here, and I'm grateful for the pain that keeps me here." I finally understand what he meant.

I treasure those precious words, and I keep them locked tight in a sturdy safe of fewer regrets. At any rate, I look forward to our future gatherings. Thank you for your valued time and your considerate attention. Be well, Suzy. Love and Respect to You.

Sincerely (your new friend),

William P. Hyneezitzs

LOST AT THE BAR

Confessions of the Drunk and Stupid

By D.S. Ayars

"To understand a proverb, and the interpretation; the words of the wise, and their dark sayings" (Proverbs 1:6).

"**H**ey! Solomon! Bring us another round of drinks, will you?" Jeez, in just two-in-a half hours I'll be delivering newspapers to these rude pricks. "Coming right up, Jared...Alright Omega, I need to cash in on the favor you owe me. Would you, please, take these watered-down drinks to the group of shit slinging apes over there?" If I didn't have Omega and Patience working with me, I would have burnt this wretched place down to the fucking ground, along with everybody in it, years ago. "Love to, Boss," she replies whilst she tucks the bar gun, which is never loaded, in the back of her pants. With a smile going from ear to ear, she winks at me stating, "If they touch me, or if they say anything nasty to me, I believe I have the right to shoot them." I confirm, "I'm counting on it."

I make no mistake, nobody comes in here to better themselves, their lives nor the lives of those around them. Everybody who comes here and has a drink to 'unwind' or 'have a good time' is bitter about something. 'I had a bad day' or 'it's girls' night out' are all excuses and justifications to get fucked up and fuck up — 'because I was drunk'. The bottom line is I am in the business of self-interest. Omega grabs the tray of cheap drinks and struts over to Jared's table with the confidence of somebody packing a firearm.

Jared is the partial owner of a mediocre grow-op (he's not great with money), and the poor fools getting obnoxiously intoxicated with him are his employees. Over-privileged, Jared, I'm certain, brought them here to get them drunk because he cannot pay them in full their agreed cut from the last harvest. Just like too many times before he'll charge, "We'll just have to work harder. Then after this next big harvest, I will take care of you guys," all evening, the same tired-old broken promises. What a dick.

"Here are your drinks, boys," Omega states approaching Jared's table. Flirting, Jared shouts, "Well, hello beautiful! Who do we have here?" Assuming he's cute and funny, Jared yells in Omega's face, "I've been eyeballing you all night, hot stuff, it's about time the boss sends you over!" Omega continues to serve the embarrassed party's cocktails, even Jared's, with a generous smile. She bends to reach across the table to serve the last beverage, then Jared unwittingly presumes he's entertaining the boys by making sport of Omega's ass by wiggling his tongue, bulging his eyes and pretending like he's going to grab her. He spots the butt of the gun exposed from the back of her jeans.

Jared smacks her voluptuous rump and bellows, "Is that a gun in your pants, or are you just happy to see me?" Precisely when his hand landed on her ass, the back of Omega's hand landed on the moron's face as hard as her farm girl arm could swing. And with every one of her fingers riddled with oversized, gaudy rings—she loves jewelry. BAM! Omega knocks him out, cold. In self-defense, of course. The table applauds and quickly finishes their drinks before they pick up the remains of their miserly boss, so they can drop him off to his disappointed wife and alienated children. The crew pool a nice tip for Omega from what little they make.

I ask Omega how we did for the night after she cleaned up the mess, "That was the only big party tonight, so when I knocked him out the party was over. Typical Thursday." Which is why I also have a paper route for supplemental income. It was worth it to see the million-dollar smile never leave Omega's face through the whole incident. "Could you close the bar for me, tonight?" I politely ask. "Sure," she replies with an upbeat tone. "You keep all the tips for the night, and I'll see you at the same time and place tomorrow... Thank you, Omega." "Be careful, there's people out there," she incites upon my exit.

Full disclosure, I could not tolerate running this place without Omega, or Patience. Patience only works here on the weekends when it is excruciatingly busy, and she works this old bar like a well-oiled machine. The drunk and stupid have a great time here in Solomon's Cellar, especially on the weekends. It's an awkward and infuriating paradox, however, that here in Spokane, Washington of all places, my best thinking bought this smelly old tavern, and I don't even drink.

Omega and Patience have both worked for me ever since I took over this rusty shack ten damaging years ago. Omega was raised organic. In other words, she's a farm-girl from Post Falls, Idaho. She holds all the charm, beauty, integrity, and all the rode-hard and put-away-wet strength to back it all up. Patience, on the other hand, isn't as nice as Omega. Patience shows no shame in the fact she enjoys a disturbingly deep disdain for people in general, and an even deeper disgust for those who occupy their time with drunkenness and debauchery. She's big, black, and beautiful. I might be in love with her, but I respect her too much to damage our good standing with something so childish as a crush. They are the smartest investments I've ever made, even regarding this bar. Omega and Patience are my best friends.

Friday is nipping at my calloused heels, and I need to get this perfidious paper route over with so I might sneak in a couple hours of sleep—whatever that is. 'No rest for the wicked' they say, so I must have done something terribly wrong. I started slinging paper ten years ago for supplemental income, but now I need it. Not for cash. In the realm of finances, I'm solid. Just in case, though, my parents are rich. Now, the paper route is more of a way to come down from the ugly buzz and the freakishly sticky angst I accumulate catering to the self-interested, the megalomaniacs and the narcissists.

As crazy as it is, I know full well I'm addicted to addicts, which makes me a fool. A fool with a bar. It's sick, the self-righteous intoxication I reap from quietly condemning the hideous and grim words and deeds of the creeps who keep my business thriving. What a screwed-up and twisted symbiotic relationship. Not unlike my brother and me. As far as William is concerned, I am extinct, and in return I look down on him for being a ridiculously wimpy dumbass. A clinical psychologist with no coping skills, what an overdeveloped denial mechanism.

In part, I keep the bar and sling paper so I can continue to feel superior to his weak ass, I can feel more successful because he's too mentally timid to work. If there wasn't any of this meaningless bullshit between us, I would sign this bar over to Patience and Omega in a second. I would certainly stop doing this perfidious paper route. Unfortunately, it too has run its course and enraged my cynicism and dislike for folks these days. I used to like people. But, in the darkest hours of the night, some creatures will do some of the most heinous things, some of the most atrocious shit, when they think nobody can see what they are doing.

I suppose I would just start writing full time. At any rate, I ought to deliver the bad news so everybody has something to look forward to when they get up, and so I can sneak a brief nap in before the big payday, Friday. Saturday pays even better. Friday and Saturday night are the nights my regular alcoholics and addicts get warped. Most of them are broke by Sunday, either way they all pay heavily in one way or another. They come in with entitlement written all over their faces, because as far as they're concerned, they've earned what happens next. As it stands, I still can't make any sense out of the foolishness of it all. Repeat ad nauseam.

One consistent and certain thing I can always count on is the meticulous work ethic I enjoy with Patience and Omega. They are two of the most reliable people I've had the perfect pleasure to know and work alongside. Patience and Omega open and close the bar for me on the weekends. This arrangement affords me some rest, and it affords them some financial assurance. "Hey, Solomon, what's up?" Patience welcomes upon my entering the Warzone at six pm, sharp—just like every Friday and Saturday night. "Hey, Boss!" Omega cheerfully greets.

They are always close at hand every time I arrive, typically this is so they can give me my orientation to the foul activities and the destructive behaviors going on within my bar. "How are you two masters of the universe doing this evening?" I quickly return, while

I brace myself for the ugly report. Omega perks up, and with her sparkling smile states, "Patience finally threw the weird couple out of the bar for good, you know, the Wills? The freaky couple who have been frequenting the bar, all summer long. Every time they come in rolling on molly, then after a few glasses of expensive wine and lame-ass repetitive conversations, they both keep sneaking into the men's bathroom to offer blowjobs for OxyContin or coke. Both of them." Her eyebrows raise with an even more robust smile.

"Danny and Kate? Yeah, I know who you are talking about. Sometimes they'll do it for a free drink," I accidentally return. "You are going to have to get your sleazy sucks elsewhere now, Solomon," Patience intervenes for a moment. "Well," Omega continues, "Patience was booting them out, this time for good, and Kate ran out embarrassed, but Danny, instead, tried to bargain with Patience. Patience yelled, 'Shut your cocksucker!' while she spun him around towards the exit and literally kicked him in the ass. While he staggered to keep his balance on the way out, he shouted back to Patience, 'I think I'm in love with you!' Then finally, they ran off into the sunset with their proverbial tales between their legs. It was hilarious as hell!" Omega convinces with a jolly laugh that, for a moment, lights up the atmosphere.

"I sure as fuck, hope those two do not breed, because the turd doesn't fall far from the asshole," Patience concludes on the matter. Well, the night is still young, and the weekend attracts the most slippery of sleaze to this bar. So, I anxiously expect the best is yet to come. Tonight is 'just a few of my friends are getting together' and 'just us girls are going out for a bit, be back soon' night, an excused time to get fucked-up, reckless and unaccountable. For most of mediocrity, this is totally normal behavior. Patience, Omega, and I know better.

Without fail, somebody from the lady's group is licking, sucking, and fucking some moron from the guy's group. Most of the time, the moron is screwing more than one. Tonight, is not an opportune night for such menacing maneuvers. One of the lady's involved in a philandering engagement happens to be married with three children to a well-liked and highly respected officer of the law—especially amongst his co-workers.

Sgt. Freely is the African American police officer who, unfortunately, is married to the unfaithful milky-white-skinned redhead named Chance. Sgt. Freely's comrades have been surveying this mindless affair, per Freely suspecting something's off about Chance since the beginning of the summer. Incidentally, Chance and Adam (the suicidal idiot) have been enjoying an openly loose affair since the beginning of the summer. And Freely is fully aware of it. Chance and Adam haven't got the slightest clue, Freely knows.

Adam is also married with two kids of his own. Adam and his buddies yell for more shots, while Chance winks and licks her lips at him from her 'girl's night out' table. Excitedly, Omega perks up like she can sense what's going to happen next, "I've got this," she alerts Patience and me. "Here's your drinks, boys," Omega announces to Adam's table as she approaches, with her charming smile intact. Adam advances Omega, "So when are you going to let me buy you a drink? I've been coming here for a few months now. I feel like we kind of know each other. Besides, you look fantastic."

Smiling like a lit-up jack-o'-lantern, Omega responds, "If you knew me, you would know I don't drink. But what I know is you have a devoted wife who is at home, right now, taking care of your two kids, your house, and meals while you frequent our establishment every Friday and Saturday night wearing your badge of entitlement. You think you've earned the right to cheat because you think you work hard and 'nobody understands you'. So, regarding your offer, eat glass."

"Oh, what she doesn't know won't hurt her," Adam slurs. "Come on, gorgeous, good vibes only!" Omega's eyes open wide and light up, whilst she laughs hysterically, then, SMACK! From behind, Sgt. Freely slaps dumb Adam across the right ear, knocking his staggering and now confused body to the beer-stained floor. THUNK!

Sgt. Freely doctors up the score by slipping a pair of brass knuckles on, while Adam attempts to gather himself from the stupefied condition he just got himself into. None of Adam's friends bother intervening, because Freely brought five of his closest on duty, fully uniformed cop friends with him to keep guard and give moral support, so he may freely beat the adulterer to a bloody pulp. There is nothing anybody is going to say or do. Nobody to call. The police are already here.

"What the fuck?" Adam whines with a high-pitched voice, as he sits squat legged on the floor with an obnoxiously loud ringing in his head. CRUNCH! Freely lands a fist full of brass knuckle on the septum of Adam's bloody nose. Adam slams back to the ground, this time fully unconscious. Unfortunately for Adam's faculties, the beat down didn't stop there. Head wounds always bleed the worst; Patience and I look at each other with concern over the mess we will have to clean up when the correction is finally over. Sgt. Freely continues with a steel-toed kick to Adams's overactive nuts. Everybody gasps with every merciless hit administered upon stupid Adam, and yet, 'nobody saw a thing'. Omega laughs even harder.

Not once did Chance try to stop the wreckage. She kept her mouth shut and spinelessly watched the ugly consequences of her 'harmless' decisions unfold in front of a full bar of spectators. "If you didn't have kids, I'd fucking kill you right now!" Freely testifies. He throttles the last of his bone cracking blows to the dumbass and confirms, "This one is for your kids, and this one is for your unlucky wife!" Sgt. Freely stops, catches his breath, spits on Adam's bloody face and mumbles, "You rotten bastard."

Omega, still laughing, was standing directly in front of and over the whole unsettling scene, but not without reward. Sgt. Freely smiles at her while he hands her five thousand dollars in crispy $100 dollar bills as he says, "Sorry about the mess, and the hideous make-over. Stellar service, though. Thank you, Omega." He nods with a wink to Patience and me upon exiting the busy bar, with which he then turns and yells at Chance, "Don't bother coming home! I shoot strangers who try trespassing on my private property!" The other officers stay behind to assure Adam gives the medics a perfect story about a drunken accident that almost killed him, and unfortunately, can't remember how it happened. No witnesses. But it all checks out.

Not even two hours past the jarring event, and folks are drunk and high enough to poke fun at the menacing spectacle— the bloody beating. But this is the only place their jokes can ever be told without possible harsh consequences. After Omega thoroughly cleans up the mess (evidence), she gleefully walks over to Patience and me with the same sunshine smile she held during the whole beat down. "Great tips, tonight," she says, "Along with a fun conversational piece, don't you think? Solomon?"

"If you call monotony a fun conversational piece. I am so fed up with only witnessing the arrogant, the deceitful and the detestable side of everybody in the grim walls of this abomination shack," I snidely whimper with a poor-me sigh. "In fact, I only bought this fucking dump out of spite. It was all purchased out of vanity. Worse yet, I don't even think my brother cares. Sure, my bank account may be sturdy, but my soul has deteriorated. If we could reconcile, just forgive, I would give this snake pit over to you two in a second. I don't even remember what made us bitter toward each other. Either way, this bar has become the filthy security blanket I drag around while sucking the self-pity out of my thumb," I rant.

Patience rolls her eyes and chuckles, "Easy does it, bitch and moan. So, you're stuck with us and this place too. Whatever. Things could always be worse. Deal with it, champ." Adam becomes painfully conscious of what went down and what's to be said, via the expert advice of Freely's officer buddies. Just when the ambulance arrives, Adam had already been coached on what to say and when to say it at least five times before the EMTs entered the establishment. He was solid on what was next, or else. The police officers made certain the EMTs got their report. Nobody saw what happened.

Besides, Adam didn't want his wife to know why he got his ass handed to him extra shredded. In addition, the EMTs didn't care what happened either way. They are so calloused to all the bar accidents they have to pick up every weekend, the EMTs almost don't even require a report anymore. Health care workers aren't common fools, they know full well most of the stories they gain from their patients are fictitious. After the night's high lowered to a shadowy buzz, I broke away from the demanding and loud tipsy crowd to apologize to Omega for my rude attitude towards her earlier. Patience highly recommended I do, and she is very persuasive for multiple reasons, not-to-mention her intimidating personality.

"Omega, I'm really sorry about being so rude to you after you cleaned up that big mess, tonight," I say to her with all sincerity, "Will you please forgive me?" Omega's smile drops to an open-mouthed inquiry. With a shrug of her strong shoulders she questions, "What the fuck are you talking about? I have heard nothing rude from your sweet mouth, all night, Solomon." All I can gather in response to this kind of grace is, "You are the best, thank you, Omega." In the same moment I turn and yell to Patience, "You too, Patience!"

Patience looks at me with a smirk and yells back, "What the hell are you shouting at me, you asshole?" I stroll over to her and say, "Thank you," as I open my arms for a hug and continue to walk towards her. She glares and declares, "Oh, you had better step back creep or I'll drop you like a lead turd." She doubles up her fist and caulks it back, then raises her eyebrows with disdain to assure authenticity of threat. I stop and put my arms down, "I am just grateful for you and Omega. I just wanted to express it somehow." Patience busts up. In fact, she folds over with uncontrollable laughter.

Omega comes to my embarrassing rescue, "It's almost two o'clock, shouldn't you go deliver the bad news?" I cling to what little dignity I can muster up and return, "You are absolutely correct, what would I do without you two?" Hoping to control a different reaction from Patience. She looks up at me only to laugh even harder. "Okay, I'll see you two tonight," I sarcastically finish with, "Saturday! I can't wait to see what tonight has in store for us." Patience is able to conclude through her merriment, and at the same time as Omega, "Have a good night, boss."

I deliver the papers and when I get home (around six a.m.) I obsess on my lifelong grudges and nurse myself to sleep in self-righteous indignation. This daily ritual lasts until two or three in the afternoon before I finally lay down to rest my spasming back and crooked neck. My mind never shuts the fuck up, and it's pissed-off. When my alarm clock screams at me around four or four-thirty, depending on how many times the snooze button entices me, I slither out of bed and follow a strict regimen of getting ready for my day in a timely manner. I am at the bar every day by six p.m., sharp.

I enter Solomon's Cellar at six o'clock on the dot, eager to hear all about the Saturday night low-brow activities so far. Upon entry, I see Omega working the full tables, but no twisted story told with a twisted smile to start my night. Something is different. Patience, however, pleasantly greets me with a smile and some good news, "Good morning, Boss," she says while wiping down a beer glass, "For what it's worth, it has been a smooth night. Granted, it's busy, and the night is young, but it has been pretty cool tonight. Oh, and there is somebody here to see you. Now stop staring at me, you horse's-ass!" She ends with a quick glare.

I wasn't intending to gawk open-mouthed at her; I was just dumbfounded by her unusual kindness, which makes this visitor in question more compelling. Hell, I might just be in a good mood, I think. "Who is it?" I inquire of Patience's knowledge. "What's wrong, don't you like surprises?" She teases with a genuine smile. "She's at the end of the bar listening to Nina Simone on the old juke-box and drinking a virgin-margarita while she indulges in a joint." After giving me the mother-load clue, my bloodshot and weary eyes widen and brighten as I irrepressibly yelp in a high-pitched voice, "BellaRae!" Patience confirms, "Bingo! Alter boy! Now don't be rude, go say hi, numb nuts."

Through the dusty crowd, like a beacon of light at the end of a deep dark tunnel, there sat my sister-in-law BellaRae. She's one of my favorite people on this poisoned planet, in fact, she is one of the most respectable people I've ever had the good pleasure to know. She spots me approaching her table and begins waving at me with the enthusiasm of an old friend whom I have not seen in a long, long time. "BellaRae!" I enthusiastically shout as I open my arms for a hug.

She gets up from her seat to give me a hug with, "Please be quiet until the song is over," then squeezes me tight with loving sincerity. BellaRae has never considered music background noise, she listens. After the forty-second hug we sit while the song plays on, she takes a sip of her favorite mocktail and pulls out a fat joint, or doobie as she likes to call them, from inside of her burgundy chemise. One thing I remember about her is if she lights a doobie, you smoke it. Otherwise, you might miss out on some valuable insight and a refreshing laugh. BellaRae lights the joint, takes a long drag, then passes it to me. Amid taking a lung scorching pull, the song ends, and I cough myself into a red-faced spaz.

BellaRae cheerfully greets, "How the fuck are you, Solomon? I've missed hanging out with you!" She says, laughing at my sudden predicament. "It is great to see you under different circumstances, that is, I come bearing good news, Sol. For you, for me and for all of us. Hold on, I'll tell you after this next song is over, okay? Thank you." During our intermission to the song Double Trouble by Otis Rush, I wave Omega and Patience over to the table so they can help us finish this joint to keep me from passing out before I learn more about BellaRae's message. I don't specifically know why she came to see me; nonetheless, it is like Christmas morning having the odd opportunity to just visit with her.

After topping off the joint, Omega and Patience go back to work and the song ends, BellaRae lights another joint and picks up where she left off, "Your brother is on a steadfast path of reconciliation. Redemption. I know damn well he has hated you the most, even to the point of disowning you over the last few years. He's always been jealous of you, Sol. He's always felt like your parents treated you better than him. Also, it doesn't help that you and I had a brief love affair shortly before him and I got married. But this means you are definitely on the list, and your turn ought to be approaching very quickly.

He misses you. I miss you and your nieces and nephews miss you. The only reason Pops calls you back for another newspaper every other day is because he wants to see you. And though your interactions are strained, as far as he's concerned, at least he got to see you. To know you are okay. He is working hard to figure out the right words and the right time to present an amends to you," she stops to finish her drink. BellaRae then takes a couple of drags from the still burning joint. "That's all I've been waiting for," I self-righteously proclaim.

She goes on with her accurate assessment, "Fug, Solomon! Deranged. Wait, after this song." Damn music fiend, I need her to elaborate. I know she will look out for my best interest with whatever she says next, I'm just eager for her to tell me how to let go of the fierce grip I have on this bag of torment. And through the song Sultans of Swing, it slugs me, I've forgotten how to forgive. I've refused for so long. I've fostered hatred and bitterness, I've consciously opted to deny myself, and my family, love, and friendship.

The song fades to a close and I'm daunted by my realization. BellaRae returns to her professional observations, "You bought this bar and let it deform you into this crusty grudge creature, all this time, out of spite. You need this just as much as Pop does." My impatience presses, "Need what?" She gets directly to the point, "Okay dumbass, the time has come and is ripe for a good outcome regarding you and Pops finally reconciling. All that's left is to let a little light through your assholes so you two can see what the next right move is. Don't be sorry, Solomon, be considerate. It will change your life."

"Guilty-ass-charged, BellaRae," I resolve. "You are right, I'm ready to shed this heavy load of resentment. I have to admit, though, I am more afraid of letting go of this bar than I thought I was. I've promised Patience and Omega, multiple times through the years that when this day comes, I would turn the bar over to them. I'm ready to make things right with my brother, but the bar has been a place of identity for me for so long. Here, I've felt in charge, in control. My position has afforded me a sense of superiority over the lost folks who have come here, religiously, and have paid my bills with their compulsions. What do you recommend?"

Whatever BellaRae suggests will be the right thing to do, I am certain of this. "First," she begins, "It is absolutely imperative you stick to your word, for good or ill. Consistency is the key on this front, for your wellbeing and the welfare of those around you. So, when you and Pops make amends, don't let your best friends down. Indeed, Patience and Omega have been your family for the last few years, they've faithfully been there for your miserable ass. Solomon, you don't need this place anymore. They've never lost their way here, and they've always helped you find yours."

BellaRae strikes again, "Second, it is time for you to stand upright and re-establish a proper relationship with your alienated family. It's responsible to be accountable, and that is all long lasting, good stuff. Here's the plan: Tonight, when you are doing the paper route, save our stop for last. But after you drop our paper off on the driveway, park at the end of the street, out of sight. It will be approximately eight thirty in the morning, so it shouldn't be but a few minutes before Pops calls for another newspaper."

I begin to feel anxious and a tad reluctant, but BellaRae soothes my tensions, "Upon arriving, just park your car and come on in. I will have a big breakfast for us, prepared for a good time of burying the hatchet. A clean slate, once and for all. At any rate, it has been a true treat hanging out with you tonight, Solomon. Now would be a perfect time to go get Patience and Omega, so you can share the good news to the new owners of this establishment, while we smoke this last doobie."

Patience and Omega somehow knew what the news was, BellaRae's presence made it obvious, I think. Either way, it was about time. They deserve a bar of their own. We celebrated quickly because I had to get to my route. After BellaRae left, I ask Omega and Patience on my way out, "If I need a job, can I come and work here?" Both of them answer emphatically, "Fuck no!" I'll never get lost at the bar again.

After I finish my route, I drop off the last paper at the Hyneez-itzs home and then park at the end of the street, out of sight. It's eight thirty in the morning, I'm exhausted, excited, and scared. I wait. Ten minutes, twenty minutes and thirty minutes go by. My mind twists, turns and gets down right mean. "This was a huge mistake," I angrily fuss out loud to myself. Pissed-off, I decide I will drive by their house, honk my horn, and flip them off. "Fuck you!" I bellow out loud to myself as I mindlessly plot out the plan.

I slow down as I approach their driveway only to see my brother standing there, facing me with a big smile, and holding up the newspaper I'd delivered to him forty minutes ago. After he waves me in, I park and shut the car off. Pops opens my car door and says, "You're just in time for breakfast, come on in where it's warm." As we walk up the steps of his home, Pops pats me on the back and states in a genuine and kind tone, "It's really good to see you, Solomon."

BELLARAE
Quiet Please, Psychedelic Session in Progress

By: D.S. Ayars

"For myself, these experiences have been most strange, most awesome, and in their own way amongst the most beautiful in my life" (Dr. Humphry Osmond).

To expand the mind's awareness is the dictionary's definition or explanation of the term, or the experience psychedelic. Curiously enough, as pedestrians we are wondering trappings of poly-chemicals, thereby leaving us with the rigid realization we are, for good or ill, mind-altering substances. What we do and say matters. In the bizarre realm of psychedelics, I, being a psychiatrist and schooled musician, enjoy these kinds of sessions on a consistently welcomed basis. In my many years of practice and expertise, I've discovered these types of expansions remain transient to the fearful and the lazy. But, when my courageously hard-working rag-tag band, Painful Pleasure played at Baldo's Bar and Grill, in Redding, California for the 1969-1970 New Year's Eve party, this place was home to one of my invaluable experiences of expanding the mind. An astounding odyssey, indeed.

And those of us who were in attendance to this celebration certainly did revel in it. Now the mind may very well be the principal character in this loud account, however, I am bound by sentiment to the degree that I find it my duty to describe the participants of this fiercely fun occasion. I was seventeen; I was pretentiously talented; I was angry and ready to go right for the nuts of this spinning circle. I was thrilled for my band to play one of these Baldo New Year's Eve parties, though. But I was more anxious than usual for this particular show because this would be the first time I took L.S.D.

Baldo was one of the sincerest and generous kind folks I'd met in the satanically sweltering town of Redding, California. Baldo had this graciously pleasant presence about him, even with the unexpected deviant sparkle in his ganja flushed eyes. The deviant sparkle exposed how he'd tapped into an inner beast, one, maybe one hundred times before, and the consequences left him humbled to the decent guy I had always known him to be. I was introduced to Baldo by my good friend and fellow music nerd, Bob. Bob was my right-hand man in our unconventional band, and nobody kept still whenever he would play his six-stringed axe. One could note upon meeting Bob, he was just visiting a planet unworthy of his presence.

At any rate, the idea jelled when Bob, John and I were working on a music project together, approximately two months before the soiree—we branded the progressive works Muzak for Good or Ill. It just so happened Bob had been visiting Baldo at his spacious and charming home, when Baldo curiously suggested to Bob that he should have his band come and perform our 'far-out' music at his upcoming New Year's Eve party. As a result, Bob asked John and

I if we would do such a thing for a good guy like Baldo. Without hesitation we answered, "yes."

Before getting into the landscape of the whole thing, a quick note regarding this mutant, John. John was an ominous drummer, but more importantly, he was my good buddy. Thorn-head was his self-proclaimed handle. John was a good guy in disguise, and frankly, the world didn't deserve his gifts and talents. He hid his deep love for others, and he kept caged in the dark corners of his mind an Olympic-styled bigot. But this kept old Thorn-head in a constant state of creative flux. I loved John's schooled talents just as much as I miss the irritated, fun-loving bastard. When he played those drums, it was like being caught in the middle of a raging mid-summer storm, excitingly brilliant. All the while, one must keep enough healthy fear to not get too close, or you will get hit by one of those high-wattage volts and know full well your life has been transformed. Hence, John, my drummer and good friend, in a nutshell.

The same day of the party, after our collaborated confirmations, without delay or resistance, we set out to place our equipment in its proper place for the shindig. Everything arranged with ease and little effort, as if something predestined this moment in time for those who were to fill it. Baldo's spacious home was simple to prepare for a successful delivery of hospitality. His facility offered a fully functioning wet-bar thirsty for exploitation, three large grills ravenous to sear the high-quality meats for the festivities of the night, and a big screen television in every corner to captivate any saturated soul dumbfounded by the whole spectacle. In addition, to fine tune the whole space, he played splendid music through his skull cracking sound system.

The loud jazz filled the house and ruminated through the heated patio where the dutiful pool table stood next to the dance floor and the spectator chairs. This is where Bob, John and I were to dictate our alien grooves to the freaks of the night, all three of us quietly and nervously keeping in mind each one of them are eager for a good-fucking-time. After the band completed setting up our equipment, we polished, obsessively tuned, and spit words of encouragement onto our individual instruments. Our banner Painful Pleasure we put on display behind and above our fortress of amps.

Baldo was cautious to invite and alert the surrounding neighbors in his well-to-do neighborhood, in order to avoid any twitchy complaints, or 911 phone calls that would disrupt our friendly gathering. Which was the last loose end to tie this thing together. The band and I went to our collective dwellings to prepare ourselves for this anticipated night. Baldo began composing his legendary barbeque delights, consisting of melt in your mouth tri-tip, juicy steaks, and sloppy ribs. All of which would be garnished with universal side dishes accompanying the mind-numbing drinks, at the disposal of any voracious alcoholic to indulge gluttonously and indiscriminately. If anybody were to leave this party sober or hungry, it would be their own damned fault.

Getting ready for the celebration was incredibly special for me on this night. It wasn't about the makeup or the clothes, getting wasted or playing the social game. Of course, I was excited to show off the band and the music we had written and worked so rigorously on. Preparation, for me, required mental endurance because this would be the first time I ever dropped acid.

I had been reading a good preponderance of literature regarding the effects and aftereffects of the substance, from experts of experience like Dr. Humphry Osmond and Dr. Duncan David Blewett. I'd also been in the throws studying the writings of C.G. Jung, Ken Kesey, and a bit of Hunter S. Thompson. I was curious about lots of things, curious enough that I held a gritty conviction to go over the edge and investigate. As a result, through the standard black-market channels (a friend of a friend, etc.), I was able to obtain three fresh hits of Owsley's acid.

I started feeling a bit of unexpected anxiety after I put on just a skosh of accent makeup, which made sense since I rarely like to wear misleading products. Either way, I was suddenly uneasy, which is not a welcome mix with high-powered psychedelics. However, if this was to be part of the trip, so be it, I reconciled. But thiswas not necessarily my design for the night at hand.

My attire was stress free with a pair of bell-bottom blue-jeans, a long sleeve purple sweater, and a matching purple bandanna because I love Jimi Hendrix. Physically, I was totally prepared for the bash, so I grabbed my trusty bass guitar, sat down on my bed, and warmed up with a couple of drills to loosen up and focus. Finally, after about forty-five minutes, I took a few psych-out breathes, said another prayer, and placed the high-quality substance on my tongue—all three of the tabs. As I wiped down my bass and put it in its case, I could feel the L.S.D. disintegrate in my mouth. The inside of my mouth felt like it was floating, and slowly, the floating sensation (which was sensational) made its way throughout my entire body. It slowly intensified into a fascinating electric vibration, a colourful frequency.

Time became insignificant, because after I dropped the acid it seemed like Bob called immediately to see if I was on my way, yet. I was definitely on my way. On the phone, Bob said John, and he was already at the party destination warming up for our set. I assured my enthusiastic guitarist my ride was in route to pick me up for the festivities at hand. Directly after I hung up the phone with Bob, John called. His inquiry was exactly the same as Bob's.

It was unanimous; I was frying balls, and I needed to get to my bandmates at once.

I was getting the fear and in this state of mind there was no asking my parents for a ride, besides, they were already out and about for the holiday. And just before I got locked into another rabbit hole, my rich friend Suzy drove into the driveway. "Finally!" I angrily shouted to myself, as if my ride were late. Quite the contrary, she was actually a little early regarding the time we'd planned for her to pick me up. Along with a couple more of her over-privileged friends, Suzy's clique.

Suzy and I grew up together. In fact, we met when we were only five years old in Sunday-school. We've been friends ever since—close friends. We have been through a great deal together. Miraculously, I've been able to convince Suzy out of four different suicide attempts within the last ten years. Thus, one of the many reasons I pursued psychiatry, and my own family dynamics being another.

Suzy's other well-off friends wanted me in their loop because I was a shiny novelty for them, and I was popular for the right reasons, so I broke up the horribly boring monotony of their limited world. At any rate, they'd shown up in plenty of time to get to the party, and for that I was profoundly grateful. Unfortunately, Suzy and her friends also dropped acid, but they were drinking Jack Daniels and snorting coke too. This was my designated driver, moreover, these were my so-called invited guests—what a crazy little ship of fools.

I was already committed to the plan; I didn't feel like I had much choice in the matter, so I got in the self-destructive vehicle and we swerved off to the Hooten-Anny. They hollered and slurred rants of pomp the whole way, with the radio playing perfectly delightful music even. The dreadfully irritating part was nobody could hear it over their narcissistic fits of snide. Fortunately, the party was only three miles from my house, yet it seemed like it took hours to get there. This clique had no self-awareness, only great expectations of getting wasted and overlooking any scraps of self-respect and dignity.

Surprisingly, we showed up to the destination physically unharmed. At exactly five thirty p.m., December thirty-first, 1969, we landed at Baldo's Neighborhood Bar and Grill New Year's Eve party. Baldo, the gracious host of the festivities this night, was diligently serving a tsunami of strange, twisted, and sharp-dressed guests. All this and he still greeted us at the door. 'Gracious host' was unequivocally the proper nomenclature to describe this hospitable proprietor. Nobody attending the celebration was in need, nor want for that matter. Baldo tended to and acknowledged every attendee without his red eyes losing sight of anybody, nor did he break an anxious sweat. He was a third-degree black belt in throwing a party, the maestro of this domain.

Upon entering this funhouse, directly to the left of me stood a tall industrial-sized refrigerator bursting full of crispy cold sodas along with sweet and sour juices for mixing hard drinks, daring everybody to open its doors and take hold of anything a parched soul could desire. However, the first thing to catch my ears were the four-shining pin-ball machines right next to the mammoth cooler, clattering and clanging abrupt jingles, and shoving bright lights in front of anything I tried to focus in on. After turning away from the cold drinks, the flashy games, and recapture my vision, there sat the eloquently prepared feast. The meal filled the whole dining room.

The sights and smells were so brilliant; I could taste each dish without taking a single bite. If food and games were not appealing to a party-pooper, one could simply take a right and follow on through and take route to the wet bar in the primary room. The living room displayed a movie screen playing A Christmas Carol, and on the opposite side of the room was a daunting fireplace made stone by stone, laughing hysterically with flames of mirth. A proudly prodigious saltwater tank full of odd-looking tropical creatures stood next to the elated fireplace. Despite the realization that at least fifty extra guests more than had been invited began to show up, there was still plenty of finely cushioned leather seating to cradle the uninvited patrons.

Between the fireplace and the wet bar was an opened sliding-glass-door leading to the heated, family-reunion sized patio. Ironically, for me, the opened door was my official entrance. The stage was my domain, and though I was tripping hard, I was excited to take my post. My sanctuary—my comfort zone. This was where my band-of-gypsies were to minister amusement to the freaks and friendly fiends who attended this remarkable event.

It was around 8:30 p.m. when the acid shined its terrible flashlight on my unconscious contents and processes—the L.S.D. made its way to the dark corners of my mind—causing the bizarre mingling of the sixty plus festive assemblage to become one unified loud sound, like unrelenting white noise. Everything and everybody appeared to be exploding with living colors. I trembled from the atmospheric pressure of all the good folks encompassing each other to indulge in and gnaw on the copious amounts of THC, psilocybin, L.S.D. and hard drinks.

And as tanked and tossed as most people were getting, not once did anybody cause harm or bring trouble to another the entire night through. But finally, I felt a bit of relief when I spotted Bob and John finding their way through the labyrinth of party animals, to the empty stage where I'd been residing. They stood around me and delivered the verdict, "It's time," my bandmates declared. "All these people want to hear us perform, now."

My overactive mind took a menacing turn, and an unforeseeable fear seized my pseudo-limber brain, "It's getting late, what if the police shut us down because of a noise complaint?" My L.S.D. soaked thoughts sprinted into a frenzy of WHAT IF games, and the timid paranoia was merciless. "For fuck-sakes," I thought, "The air is saturated with the scents of fine-dining, heavy drinking and skunky herbal remedies." The smells were so rich and robust everybody could taste it, and certainly not be able to walk away from it in a straight line.

Bob, being the tenable one he was, offered some solace with these encouraging words-of-wisdom, "This is a damn party, BellaRae, we are supposed to run-amok. These are the rules of engagement for this engagement." His concise words spilled out from his mouth like he had an acute case of the exactlys, which quickly outwitted my anxieties. We moved with the tenacious arrogance of Ludwig Van Beethoven and confidently buckled into our collective instruments. Once we were armed and dangerous, Baldo made the announcement.

And though I was in a paranormal state without a green card, with astounding success we hit a home run with our strangely danceable tunes. John always claimed, "If we can get the ladies dancing, well, then we are a hit." Subsequently, accompanied by the low lion growl of my excited bass, the smooth tickle and bite of Bob's guitar, and the ominous elephant stampede of John's percussion, the ladies were indeed dancing. The more the applause, the better we sounded.

However, just like a self-fulfilling prophecy, approximately five songs deep into our good time, the police showed up at the party due to a nerve-racked noise complaint. Our gleeful gathering eventually made somebody nearby uneasy. The officers were oddly far from objectionable about the activities of our holiday festivities. Quite the contrary, the four police officers ultimately had us finish our set with the volume slightly turned up, which was at least seven more songs.

Law enforcement stayed for those seven songs to smoke out with us and have a beer—or two. Until this very day, as much as I have studied on it, I couldn't begin to fathom what brilliant linguistic skills or what appealing bartering tools Baldo used to keep Redding's finest, graceful. Because none of the police officers who were at the party (because of the noise complaint) treated us like we were criminals, or like they were cops. We all had a fantastic time.

The night fell into eleven-thirty p.m.; we had finished our set for at least an hour. Regardless of how much fun we enjoyed, I was relieved we were done, because I was head-long over the edge in a psychedelic frenzy. But like a good hallucination, Bob and John confronted me again with a new regimen of instructions, "Everybody wants us to do an encore after the New Year countdown," they told me. It was official, I was outnumbered, and the facts catapulted me into a second wind. I remembered the reason I took part of this thing was to contribute to the celebration, not get carried away and lost in a high.

Under proper party etiquette and in honor of a thrilling shindig, locked and loaded, we held fast our poise to deliver. We'd performed on more grandiose stages, in front of larger and louder crowds, but this was different. This was more about sharing a good time, a small vacation. A brief moment to catch our breath and glimpse at the beautiful things we've overlooked every overwhelmed day. Which was what my flaky fears were losing sight of for a short time.

At first, I didn't think I could perform in this condition—it caught me in a full-throttle peak. Be that as it may, first and foremost, we were here to play music—our music. After Bob and John escorted me back to my post in front of the microphone and draped my bass on me, they got the crowd jazzed up for our title song, Painful Pleasure. The instant we started playing, I felt right at home. I was comfortable behind my instrument, and therefore, I was confident.

All the monsters-of-rock listened intently while I declared the lyrical sage alongside our mammoth Muzak,

"Sex, drugs, rock-and-roll; religion, work, and anything political.

The love, the hate; the plans and the fate. The false, the facts; the twisted and the straight.

Life! Is a painful pleasure... Right? Here and now!

(Humanity's) Thorn! In the flesh... Painful pleasure.

The highs, the lows; the friends and the foes. The popular opinions, and the things nobody knows (or do you?). Here! And now; the future and the past. The limited perspective, the profound and the vast.

Life! Is a painful pleasure... That's right! Here and now!

(Humanities) Thorn! In the flesh... Painful pleasure."

Awaiting us on the other side of the encore, were the creatures of the night generously roaring with an avalanche of applause and whistles. I was absolutely overwhelmed, all I felt was a lot. Nineteen hundred and seventy was upon us, and it was time for me to find some solitude with my new insights and overlooked gratitude. I didn't bother collecting my rich friends, I already knew they were up to no good, and I wanted to get home quietly and safely. Baldo found a sober and trustworthy ride for me.

After consulting with Bob and John about gathering our equipment the next day, we concluded with sincere and warm New Year hugs. I buckled up for the hugs I would have to give on the way out as well. As my sober ride and I were leaving the scene, along with a heavy dose of hugs and comrade, a revelation rattled my rusty cage, and I could champion a spark of comprehensive consideration. "I am home already," I thought, "I never need to use people, places or things to realize my happiness, security and sanity." All of this dancing offers the infinite option of a conscious contact to a more excellent way.

Like the finality of the loss of a loved one, life comes at us fast and hard with its consistently changing colors, its pot-pourri of sweet smells and foul stench, which makes it even more critical to bite into and gnaw on the bitter-sweet taste of what's truly meaningful. What's genuinely important, what really matters. My driver dropped me off at my house, safe and sound. I tiptoed in to see my folks had fallen asleep watching television, so I covered them each with their own blanket and gently kissed each one of them on the cheek. I whispered, "Goodnight Mom and Dad, I love you," before I headed up to my bedroom.

After I got undressed and ready to lie down for the night, the enthralling layers of contemplation regarding my L.S.D. trip flooded my thoughts. "What did I learn?" I challenged myself out loud in order to spark some sort of purposeful analysis. I didn't want this peculiar drug, nor this spectacular night to go to waste as just another memory lost in the good-old days. While quick flashing images continued to appear, disappear, and reappear in my mechanical mind, I felt more secure in a conclusion that has, until this day, brought me much comfort and serenity. What's now obvious struck me as an unearthed mystery, while my eyes rapidly blinked into a vivid slumber.

I've discovered psychedelics come in many differing forms, yet we all cherish the same goal of a richer, fuller, and concretely complete life. Through rigorous experiences and observation, it is easy to conclude we make certain of our enrichment in reading and writing. We pray and meditate, and in like manner, we recognize inspiration through the arts. And though I use these valuable gifts to progress in worth and value, I find music is my salve, my therapy and comfort. I've discovered music always understands.

I am deeply thankful I am a musician. Music is a sure method of comforting the afflicted. Music's patterns realized within the beats and rhythms, the frequencies, and vibrations where melodies methodically dance along to the soothing motion, we all take for granted, yet completely rely upon. Consistent bubbling of a crispy clear brook, or a summer breeze blowing through a leafy tree providing shade from the blistering sun. The Muzak of rain on a rooftop, or the sound of the bizarre silence under a heavy snowfall. The roar of a rushing river, or a monstrous crowd at a damn good concert.

The music which keeps the throbbing road dictator within pumped with rage, while driving amongst other assholes. A suspenseful climax gripping an eye-closing choke hold on the one who paid good money to see the thriller, or horror movie. A song a loved one, and you shared, leaving you with fond yet sad memories. Or a personal power-song which compels one toward the greater good and a stronger sense of personal grit. Because there undeniably is a more excellent way.

It turned out the seventies were a great decade for excellent music. Moreover, it was one of those moments in history chalked full of good times and celebrations for any occasion. We had warmer hearts and thicker skin. A time of sincere friends, fun families, and closer communities. Neighbors knew each other back then, we listened to records and to one another. We laughed together, and we helped each other out with whatever, which would always lead to another neighborhood celebration.

In the end, if it is something that urges your considerations closer to the unveiling of a better, more conscientious, and wiser you, foster it. Many years of experience and critical scrutiny have taught me this for certain, wherever there is music, along with it there is always some sort of dancing. Therefore, sing beautifully, play skillfully, dance gracefully, and stay tuned. Because, in short, to establish a successfully valued set, one must leave on a good note. Selah.

ACKNOWLEDGEMENTS
Great Thanks to the Honor Roll:

John Aspling

Donovan A. Ayars

Jourdan Ayars

Sebastian Ayars

Veda Ayars

Bob Baldo

Dr. Cameron

Dr. Curtis

Farmer D.

Andrew *Dankovychart* – Cover designer & Illustrator

Andrew L. Davis

Bob Deskins

Janna Gasper

Roger Gasper

Christopher Michael Harding—Editor, and wielder of the red shame stick.

Rachael Harding

Ronda Laveen

Dr. Lippert

Bojan and PixelStudio

Amber Rayne Tindall

Gabe Tindall

Lisa Walter

Casey Wild

David Wild

Linn Wild

Sandy Wild—"Give her the reward she has earned, and let her works bring her praise at the City Gate" (Proverbs 31).

Briana Shea Williams

Tim Williams